3.

D1526412

Such a Good Girl and Other Crime Stories

Other Five Star Titles
by Ed Gorman:

Night Kills

Such a Good Girl and Other Crime Stories

Ed Gorman

With an introduction by Richard Laymon

Five Star
Unity, Maine

Copyright © 2001 by Ed Gorman
Introduction copyright © 2001 by Richard Laymon

All rights reserved.

Additional copyright information on page 243.

Five Star First Edition Mystery Series.

Published in 2001 in conjunction with Tekno Books and Ed
Gorman.

Cover design by Carol Pringle.

The text of this edition is unabridged.

Set in 11 pt. Plantin.

Printed in the United States on permanent paper.

Library of Congress Cataloging-in-Publication Data

Gorman, Edward.
    Such a good girl and other crime stories / Ed Gorman ;
with an introduction by Richard Laymon.
        p.   cm.
    Contents: All these condemned — A girl like you — The
way it used to be — A new man — Judgment — Ghosts —
That day at Eagle's Point — Such a good girl — Aftermath
— Eye of the beholder — Angie.
    ISBN 0-7862-2998-5 (hc : alk. paper)
    1. Detective and mystery stories, American.
PS3557.O759 S83 2001
813'.54—dc21   00-051069

This one is for my friend and colleague
Mary Powers Smith.

Table of Contents

Such A Good Writer by Robert Laymon 9

All These Condemned 14

A Girl Like You. 45

The Way It Used to Be. 59

A New Man. 78

Judgment 87

Ghosts. 95

That Day at Eagle's Point. 106

Such a Good Girl 126

Aftermath 162

Eye of the Beholder 190

Angie. 223

Such A Good Writer

by Richard Laymon

If you choose to read this introduction before embarking on your journey into the actual stories in *Such a Good Girl and Other Crime Stories*, thanks. Let me assure you, I won't give away any secrets about the stories. You're safe with me. In that regard, anyway.

We'll start off with a quote.

"Good books are always moral, contrasting how we are with how we should be. And the good writer knows how to do this without letting on." That's from *Wake Up Little Susie*, by Ed Gorman, the author of this collection.

Though Ed doesn't preach or "let on" that he is contrasting how we are with how we should be, it's there in every short story and novel he writes.

He seems to have, in the words of Robert Frost, "A lover's quarrel with humanity."

In story after story, we see Ed in the background shaking his head, muttering an occasional wisecrack, sometimes seething with rage, and maybe sometimes weeping over the way his characters, such real people, hurt each other.

I hear Ed's low, sad, wry voice in every sentence he writes. He seems, so often, to be asking, "How can these miserable bastards behave this way to other people?"

He hates how they act, but he seems to love them all—even the miserable bastards.

Good or bad, in Ed's eyes, they're all just people. We're all just people. He writes (in *Wake Up Little Susie*), "Good men don't go around murdering people. Sometimes bad people are good people too. Or good people can do bad things. Life is like that sometimes."

Life is like that sometimes.

More often than not.

The people in Ed's stories—parents, kids, lovers, cops, criminals, victims or others—are just ordinary folks. Most of them are struggling along the best they can in a world of fading dreams and hopes.

And most of them—in the best traditions of noir fiction, literary fiction and life itself—are screwed.

They're screwed by fate. They're screwed by pettiness. They're screwed by selfishness. They're screwed by pride and greed and envy. They're screwed by ignorance. They're screwed by their own bad choices of action, and by the bad actions of others.

When we read Ed's fiction, we feel the sadness of it all.

But Ed also reminds us regularly of how wonderful life really is. Even if most of us (or all of us) are screwed—man, how about a summer morning when you're a kid and you're just setting out on your bike? How about the way the wind smells just before a rainstorm? How about the first time you dared to take hold of a girlfriend's (or boyfriend's) hand? How about joking around with a buddy? How about the smile on your kid's face?

A lover's quarrel with humanity.

It's a wonderful world, and what a shame that so much crap gets in the way of enjoying it. Bad enough that love so often goes unrequited, that friendships fade, that jobs get lost and careers fizzle out, that we so often lose those we love and that all of us have a rendezvous with death at some forgotten barricade—bad enough, so why do we make matters even worse with petty or vicious behavior against each other?

That's what Ed seems to be asking (in the background) of all his stories, not only in *Such a Good Girl and Other Crime Stories* but in his many other short stories and novels. He is known and highly respected as an author of crime fiction, westerns, horror, political thrillers, science fiction and suspense novels of all sorts. Regardless of the "genre" he writes in, however, the same voice shows through. The sad, caring, sometimes angry, occasionally nostalgic, often funny voice of Ed Gorman.

Yeah, funny. This introduction might make it sound as if Ed's quite a gloomy guy. He sometimes seems to be. Even while his fiction can break your heart, however, it can also break you into a belly laugh. Talking to him on the phone, I spend half my time laughing. And the humor turns up in his fiction. In his new mystery series (*The Day the Music Died* and *Wake Up Little Susie* so far), he has a running situation in which the main character is frequently ducking rubber bands shot at him by his boss—a very sophisticated, very tough female judge. And here's a sample line from *Wake Up Little Susie*: "I'd rather be a petty bastard than a dipshit." That one made me laugh out loud.

Though Ed often seems to be outraged or sad about what is happening to the folks in his stories (and in life), he also gets a bang out of good, fun, innocent, silly stuff—and he likes to take amusing pokes at petty bastards, dipshits, dummies and assholes.

Don't get the impression, here, that Ed is a comedy writer. Fiction doesn't get more grim than Ed's sometimes does. The humor is there, however, brightening things up sometimes like the sun shining through a gap in the clouds.

There are plenty of clouds in Ed's work. Dark, rainy clouds and storms . . . violence, passions running amok, obsessions ruling the night . . . but there's sunlight, too. There's the bright shining example of the man or woman doing the right thing.

To borrow from William Faulkner's Nobel Prize acceptance speech, Ed writes about "the old verities and truths of the heart, the old universal truths lacking which any story is ephemeral and doomed—love and honor and pity and pride and compassion and sacrifice."

Ed Gorman's Yoknapatawpha County is the untamed wilderness of the human heart.

His stories may remind you of early John D. MacDonald. Sometimes, they may feel a bit like Winesburg, Ohio as written in collaboration between Sherwood Anderson and Jim Thompson.

But they aren't.

They're Ed.

His fiction, including the stories in this book, will sometimes break your heart, sometimes make you laugh out loud, sometimes make you angry, frequently remind you of how wonderful and painful life used to be when you were a kid, before you knew too much . . . and how nice it can still be once in a while when the sun shines through the clouds.

If *Such a Good Girl and Other Crime Stories* is your first Ed Gorman book, you'll find out what you've been missing. It's not a bad place to start. He has other story collections, however, and a great many novels you don't want to miss. I like them all, but a couple of my big favorites (in addition to those already mentioned in this introduction) are *Cage of Night* and *The Poker Club*. They're a couple you don't want to miss.

Like several other major writers of crime fiction—

including Elmore Leonard and Brian Garfield—Ed has also written some fine westerns. Whether or not you're a fan of "oaters," you might want to give Ed's a try. They're set in the old west, but they have the same qualities as his contemporary fiction. They're dark, sometimes amusing, often violent and shocking. Guess you could call them "cowboy noir."

Well, if you've actually bothered to read this introduction, thanks for bothering. Now it's time to get on with the stories.

Have a good trip.

Richard Laymon
Los Angeles

All These Condemned

Sailing to Atlantis

"Love between the ugly is the most beautiful love of all."—Todd Rundgren

1

Matt Shea always smiled when he walked into the house he'd bought his mother. It was a perfectly fine little house, a standard development little house, central air, attached garage, core appliances including self-cleaning oven and ice-making machine in the fridge.

But she'd turned it into a church. And the thing was, she wasn't of that generation. You know, you see them at mass all the time, those generations of Irish and Czech and Hispanic women for whom it was common to turn houses into shrines or grottos. Framed religious pictures everywhere. Palm drooping from behind the pictures. Crucifixes large and small throughout the house. Three or four Bibles scattered around. Holy cards on end tables. Even, on certain occasions, the scent of incense.

Incense, Matt associated with covering up the smell of grass in his college dorm room.

The funny thing was, his mother had been a regular normal human being all the time he was growing up. There was even the family suspicion that she'd had an affair or two back in the seventies when it seemed *everybody* was having affairs. She walked around in halter tops and Levi cut-offs. She liked Clint Eastwood movies. She and his father put away a goodly amount of wine most weekends, and could frequently be heard banging around on their bed upstairs while he and Don were downstairs watching sci-fi on the tube.

But then his father got a brain tumor, forty-one years old and a fucking brain tumor, and his death was so agonizing, so prolonged that Cassie just flipped out. Couldn't deal with it. Was drunk a lot. Threw up a lot. Stayed in bed and slept a lot. Anything to escape the fact that her beloved husband—and even if she had had those affairs, it was clear that she loved Rick above all others—was dying. And then he was dead and she went even more to shit, it was her college-age boys carrying her instead of the other way around, and then one day, they were never sure why, she got religion, maybe some minister she saw on TV or something, and started wearing dowdy dresses and telling the boys to watch their language and admonishing them not to practice "free love" or to use drugs. She was living in the old house at the time, the big Tudor that had been lawyer Rick's pride-and-joy, but it was too much house as the realtors liked to say, and so she sold it and put the profits in the hands of stockbroker Matt, who saw to it that she'd never have to worry about money. This being the end of the eighties, Matt was hauling ass financially, making so much in fact that he could afford to make the grand gesture of setting Mom up in her own little tract house.

The house that was now a religious shrine.

The house Matt stood in now, warmed by late afternoon May sunlight.

His mom was on the couch. She'd aged, many long years past her halter and cut-offs stage. She wore a faded house-dress, prim little white anklets, and brown—if-you-could-believe-it—oxfords. She'd gone all the way, mom, fifty-one years old, a child of the upper middle-class, now looking like a cleaning woman in somewhat ill health.

"Do you ever watch Channel 28?" she said.

His smile. "You always ask me that, Mom."

"I just think Sandy and you and the boys should make a point of watching it. You know, as a family." Channel 28 was the religious channel.

"We're pretty busy."

"You should never be too busy for God."

And just how are you supposed to respond to that?

"You're right, Mom," he said, "we should never be too busy for God."

"I just wish Sandy was more religious."

Another running battle. "She's religious in her way, Mom. She really is."

"She doesn't go to church."

"That doesn't mean she's not religious."

"She doesn't take the boys to mass. And you don't either."

"Sandy's Jewish, mom. If she attended any kind of services, she'd go to synagogue, not to mass."

"Then why doesn't she go to synagogue? There's nothing wrong with being Jewish." Mom's first major love affair had been with a Jewish kid.

"I'll talk to her about it."

"People should go to church. If they're truly good people,

16

I mean." How could the college girl who'd spent many, many long hours smoking dope and listening to Led Zeppelin possibly have turned out this way?

"I brought you something," he said. He reached in the suit coat pocket of his gray Armani and brought forth a small white jeweler's box. "I got your necklace fixed."

For her thirty-fifth birthday, Dad had given Mom a beautiful old chain necklace. But it had gotten broken and Mom had never gotten around to getting it fixed. She held it now, smiling. "I can still feel your father putting this on my neck. It was the first time he'd ever been able to afford anything really nice. He had such big fingers."

"I thought you'd like it." He leaned down and kissed her on the forehead. She was getting older, the texture and feel of her flesh was changing, and it startled him a moment. She was getting older, and just now that realization scared and saddened him. "Say, would you let me use your bathroom if I gave you a dollar?"

This was an old gag between the two of them. "Dollar-and-a-half."

"Dollar-and-a-half it is," he said. Then, as he started back toward the bathroom, "You hear from Jim lately?"

"Just the other day."

"How's he doing?"

"He says he likes his new job. I just hope he can last at this one."

Matt and Jim Shea were as different as brothers could be. Matt, handsome, self-confident, family man. Jim, pale, nervous, luckless. He'd worked sales in the computer department of a number of different local department stores. He was running out of stores. He always got fired and for reasons that were at best vague. He always seemed vaguely relieved, too. He didn't mind living in his drab little apartment on unemployment insurance. Matt was always suggesting motivational speakers Jim go see but Jim always just grinned and shook his head. Though Matt thought of himself as a major player in the world of the local establishment, Jim saw him as a just one more Mercedes-driving Nazi. Jim called a lot of people Nazis.

Matt came back after a few minutes. He'd freshened up. He had a meeting at the club with some potential investors for a small shopping mall he was trying to develop. Time for a little hairspray, a little breath spray, a few eyedrops to take the red out.

Mom was still holding the necklace when he came back. "Say hi to that brother of mine."

"I just wish you two boys got together more often."

"Oh, that'll happen as we get older, Mom. I'm sure it will."

"Why don't you take that box of paperbacks in the closet to Sandy? They're Harlequins. She reads almost as much as I do."

He smiled. "You two and your Harlequins." He said it not with contempt but with a kind of awe. He had, in his life, finished reading exactly two novels, *The Great Gatsby* and *Ethan Frome*. *Gatsby* he liked—even though the narrator sounded sort of fruity—because of the love story, which he had to admit made him tear up a time or two, him having had a terrible love affair once himself; and *Frome* he liked simply because it was short and because of the irony of the ending. Every other novel he'd "read" had come in the yellow-and-black form of Cliff Notes. He'd been a 4-point student. He just preferred non-fiction was all. He got the box from the closet, kissed his mom once again as she opened the front door for him, and was then out the door.

He liked the way the new Mercedes four-door sedan stood

so proudly in Mom's driveway. He liked the way the men and women driving home from work to their little housing development here glanced at it. Envy. That, not imitation, was the sincerest form of flattery. Envy. I want what you have. He couldn't think of a higher accolade, and hell, he'd be the first to admit he felt it, too, the way Giff McBride, ass-bandit of all ass-bandits out at the club, wheeled around in that little Brit classic car of his, Austin-Healy it was called, wheeled around and got 20% of the married women at the club to spend time with him, not to mention an even higher percentage of the waitresses, even, it was rumored, a few of the college gals who worked there during the summers. College gals, sleek and slender and sun-brown. Now that was something to *really* envy, Giff McBride being in his early fifties.

He opened the trunk and set the box of romances inside. He had to be careful not to knock over the sloshing full red can of gasoline. It had already spilled some on the newspaper it rested on. He looked at the headline. Talk about irony.

THIRD DANCE CLUB FIRE SAID TO BE ARSON
One injured seriously; two others rushed to hospital
Numbers one and two—the black dance club and then the gay dance club—one fatality each.
No fatality this time.
They'd all been lucky enough to get out alive.

He took another look at the red gas can. It looked so harmless most of the time sitting in garages to run power mowers and clean up paint spills.

But there were other uses for it, too. Yes, indeed.

2

They didn't like me much and I guess I didn't blame them. Nobody likes "experts" brought in from the outside to tell you that you're doing a lousy job.

There were four of them, detectives, two male, two female, one black, one Hispanic. They sat at a plain table in a plain room and listened to me as long as they could stand. Then their eyes would look out the window that displayed the downtown across the narrow river and they had to be thinking longing thoughts about this gentle and colorful Iowa autumn afternoon. Football weather. They could be raking leaves, playing touch football with their kids, washing the new car, or sitting in a cop bar talking about the recent union meeting about the unpaid overtime hassle with the city council.

Instead, like school children being punished, they had to sit here, a narrow room painted city-sanctioned green, listening to me play at being a psychological profiler and private investigator for a large law-firm.

While they had their own individual cases, Captain Davidson, who'd introduced me, had put them all on the arson case, which was why I was here. The arsonist had burned his third dance club to the ground three nights ago. The first fire, two people had been killed, trampled in the melee. The second fire, nobody had died, but a number of people were in the hospital. The third fire, there'd been one more fatality, a just-divorced suburban housewife out celebrating with her girl friends. An upscale downtown dance club; a gay dance club; a black dance club. No pattern.

I said, "One thing distinguishes the arsonist from other serial murderers. The typical serial killer wants direct contact with his victims. So direct that sometimes he'll reach in and take out a vital organ with his bare hands. He'll also photograph or videotape what he's done. He wants to remember the moment. He'll masturbate to it later. The arsonist, however, wants the impersonality of setting a building on fire and standing back and watching what happens. A lot of the time, he'll hide across the street so he can masturbate while watching the fire. Totally impersonal. Except for the fluid he uses to ignite the fire, he never gets his hands dirty as it were, never faces the victims. There's an interesting note here. When you look into the background of the average serial killer, you see a dysfunctional boyhood often marked by cruelty to animals. You find that with serial arsonists, too. But with them you have to add bed-wetting. We don't know why this is but from the hundreds if not thousands of cases we've catalogued, we've seen it play out time and time again."

Detective Gomez raised her hand. "Who does this arsonist think he's killing when he sets these fires?"

"Good question," I said. "I just wish I had a good answer. As we know, many if not most male serial killers have real relationship problems with females. Even killing their victims isn't enough. They'll defile the corpses—make hideous slashes and cuts in the faces, cut off breasts, mutilate the genitals. So while we don't know which female *exactly* the serial killer is destroying—a girl he is attracted to, his mother, maybe even his sister—we do know that in general he has a real problem with women.

"This particular arsonist, though, we just don't know. Even in the male gay bar there were a few dozen women. But that still doesn't tell us a lot. Based on what we know generally, we know he's angry, we know he wants to kill people, and we know that in all likelihood, he'll do this again."

Detective Henderson, who looked like the poster-boy for clean-cut WASP detectives everywhere, said, "I take it he's shy and withdrawn."

"That's probably right. Every profile I've ever seen on this kind of arsonist, he doesn't have many social skills and he's frequently unnoticed, even though he may hang around a lot.

Almost invisible in some ways."

They were paying attention now that the afternoon had gotten interactive. I should've done this earlier.

Detective Wimmers, the black man, said, "Are there any kinds of jobs this arsonist would be attracted to?"

"No job category, if that's what you mean. But they're likely to be low-level, relatively unsuccessful, whatever line they take up. These aren't aggressive people. Not usually, anyway."

Detective Holden, a red-haired, bulky man in shirt-sleeves, loose tie, and an air of belligerence, said, "What if we waste our time looking for somebody like this and it turns out he isn't anything like this at all?"

"Then he can sue the city," I said. Nobody laughed. "This is isn't an exact science. I make mistakes, no doubt about it. But generally profiling is helpful. And I think it'll be helpful to you here. Any questions?"

There weren't, of course. They just wanted out of here. All but one of them, anyway. Detective Wimmers, the black man. "Don't pay any attention to them."

I smiled. "Kind of hard not to. They always this pleasant?"

"They just don't like outsiders." He was tall, tending to beef, with a large, imposing face and a gold-toothed smile. With his red regimental-striped tie and herringbone slacks and polished black loafers with the tassles, he looked more lawyer than cop. Except lawyers don't wear guns and badges on their belts. He pinched some skin on the thick black arm shooting from his short-sleeved white shirt. "I bring my sorry black ass in here six years ago—first black detective this city ever had—and you should've heard 'em, man. Always whisperin' and jokin' and pokin' each other in the ribs. I coulda written all their jokes myself. Lots of water-melon and pork chops in the jokes, you know what I'm saying? They'd even leave notes in my locker. Death To Niggers. Shit like that."

"I'm sorry." And I was. That had to be a special hatred, to be singled out and despised that way.

"My wife and kids, they'd cry and beg me to quit. But I wouldn't, 'cause I just wanted to piss these guys off. Stay in their faces. You know what I mean? I just wore 'em down. I didn't go to the civil rights board. I didn't complain to the police review board. I just stayed in their faces. And one by one, they started bein' nice to me. The first guy, when he was nice, they started givin' him more shit than they gave me. But one by one, we started bein' friendly. And now they pretty much accept me. Our wives and kids get together. And we bowl and stuff after work. So it's pretty good here, now. And the young black cops comin' up say they aren't havin' much trouble at all, especially with the cops their own age."

"I guess I'll have to take your word for it, that these are really swell people."

He grinned with his gold tooth. "I guess they weren't real friendly, Mr. Payne. I'm sorry. Maybe if you could spend a little more time with 'em—"

He held up a manila envelope.

"What've you got?" I said.

"Photos from the crime scene. I was going over them this morning and I found something. Captain Davidson said you were going to be here the next few days consulting on the case so I thought you might want to ride along with me this afternoon. I'll tell you about it on the way."

"Fine."

3

Wimmers handed me a manila folder while we sat at a traffic light. He was a fast, savvy and aggressive driver. At one point he'd grinned and said, "You want to wear a crash helmet, fine with me."

I'd said, "And I want to make sure my insurance is paid up."

"I grew up in Chicago. My old man was a cabbie. He taught me how to drive."

I'd spent three years working out of the Chicago FBI bureau—before going private as a profiler and investigator—so he didn't need to say any more.

Just as the traffic light changed, I said, "Same guy."

"Same guy at all three fires. Just standing around watching things."

We were off. Wimmers wanted to be in the right-hand lane so we could get on the Interstate that cut through the city. God help anybody in his way.

"How many people you killed in your lifetime?" I said.

"Killed? You kidding, Payne? Hell, I've never even drawn my gun."

"Not with your gun. Your car. You didn't even notice that you ran over a couple of nuns back there."

"Yeah?" he smiled. "Serves them right for wearing black. They should wear brighter colors."

I decided to give up on my subtle drive-safely messages.

He said, "I know who the guy is."

"In the pictures?"

"Yeah. Matt Shea. Country club set. Runs his own brokerage. Lots of money, lots of clout. Reporter on the *Gazette* I know happened to notice Shea when he was filing the photos. He sent them over to me."

"Maybe Shea just likes to look at fires."

"Maybe. But what's he doing out so late, pillar of the community, family man, all that happy horseshit? The earliest any of those fires were set was 1:00 A.M."

"Good point. So where we going?"

"His brokerage."

"God, can it really be this easy?"

"Seems wrong, don't it?" he said.

"You see a guy in some photos—"

"—and you drive over to where he works—"

"—and you ask him some questions and—"

"—case is closed. And you got your man."

"I've never even *heard* of it happening like this."

"Well," he said, wheeling the police car into the parking lot of a new six-story steel-and-glass building, "there's always a first time."

The decor was designed to do one thing: intimidate you with its quiet good taste, right down to the quiet, gold-framed Rembrandt reproductions and the quiet DeBussy on the office music system. The receptionist complemented her setting perfectly, lovely in a slightly fussy and disapproving way, the only hint of earthiness or carnality found in the oddly erotic sag of her bottom inside the discreet gray Armani upscale fifty-year-olds were wearing this year.

Matt Shea did not fit quite so well into his hallowed surroundings. There was a rough-neck quality to his movements that no high-tone suit, no $125 haircut, no $25 manicure could quite disguise. It wasn't a class thing, it was a testosterone thing. He'd look rough-neck in a tutu.

He said, "Sit down, sit down."

Old-firm law school office was the motif in this particular

room, cherry wood wainscoting, built-in bookcases packed with tomes bound in leather for theatrical effect. The small fireplace snapped and popped with autumnal balm, the wood smell sweet and melancholy.

"Police, huh?" Shea said. "Wow, now this *is* a surprise." Despite his linebacker size and his big-man poise, he sounded nervous.

I didn't like him in the way you abruptly do or don't like somebody you've just met. He was too much obvious cunning and too much obvious after-shave. The perpetual overachiever who was not without a certain frantic sweaty sadness.

After we were all seated, he said, "So how can I help you?"

"Those fires," Wimmers said. He was the man here.

"Fires?"

"Dance club fires?"

"The dance club fires in the papers."

"Right."

He looked at me and shrugged his shoulders and smiled his practiced cunning smile. "Hey, I'm a family man." He winked at Wimmers and smiled. "You can ask my rabbi." He wasn't, of course, Jewish. He was just a lounge act. "I don't even go into places like those."

Wimmers carefully set the manila envelope on the desk and pushed it across to Shea. "How about looking inside?"

The smile again. He couldn't sustain it for much longer than two seconds. "You going to be reading me my rights or something?"

"I'd appreciate it if you'd just look inside the envelope, Mr. Shea."

"Sure. Be glad to."

He looked inside and then pulled the photos out one at a time. When he'd seen all three, he said, "Wow. I can see why you wanted to talk to me." He held his arms up in the air. He was still doing stand-up. "I'll come along peacefully, officer, sir."

"This isn't funny, Mr. Shea. Two people died in those fires. Another one is clinging to life."

"I was coming home. Just saw the fire trucks and stopped by."

"I see. All three times?"

"Working late. Honest. As innocent as that."

"The fires took place in different parts of the city, Mr. Shea. You take different ways home every night?"

"Fuck." Shea looked grim. He shook his head, as if chiding himself. The way you do when you've done something really dumb.

"Pardon me?"

"I said fuck," Shea snapped. "I take it you've heard the word before."

Ugly, awkward silence. Shea stared down at the two big fists he'd planted on his desk. "I didn't set those fires," he said after a while.

"I didn't say you did."

"No? You just came out here to show me these three photos but not to make any accusations?"

"I'm trying to figure out who *did* set the fires. You being there doesn't necessarily means it was you."

"It doesn't, huh?"

"No. But it may mean that you know something I should maybe know."

Shea looked at me. Fellow member of the white race. "You probably think I'm one of those candy-asses."

"Which candy-asses would those be, Mr. Shea?"

"You know. Inherited wealth. The right schools. You know something? I grew up on the west side of this city—and

27

in those days, you told people you were from the west side, they started treating you just like you were some inferior species." He looked back at Wimmers. "Something you're probably familiar with, Detective Wimmers."

Wimmers smiled sadly. "I've heard rumors about some human beings treating other human beings that way."

"You know damned well what I'm talking about. Well, that's just how it was when you were from the west side. No Choate. No Wharton School of Business. That's where my two best friends at the club went—Choate first then Wharton. But not me. I went to the community college here before I could afford the University in Iowa City. I bussed dishes there at the frat houses. All the rich fraternity boys." To me, he said, "I've worked for every dime. Every dime. And now my pathetic fucking brother goes and spoils it."

"Your brother?" Wimmers said.

"Yes, my brother," Shea said sadly. "Who do you think's been setting those fires?"

4

The middle of a vast, calm sea on a sun-golden day on a sun-golden ship. The destination was Atlantis or some other fabled land where they would know peace and security and love for the rest of their lives, where their children would prosper, and their children's children, and all would meet again in the sunny, leafy paradise that lies just beyond death.

The sound of a distant siren woke Jim Shea.

The dream vanished. The perfect dream.

Sway and jerk of moored boat. Stink of river water. Voices up on the dock. At day's end everybody with a houseboat here descended on this place. One of the last few warm days before harsh prairie winter. Most of them didn't even take their boats out. Just hauled out the aluminum tube chairs and sat there on Ellis landing listening to the Cubbies on the radio and laughing well into the work night. It was a pretty democratic place, the houseboat marina. You had lawyers talking with guys who worked on the line at Rockwell, doctors talking to guys who sold electronics stuff at Best Buys.

The boat belonged to Ella. It'd been her Dad's. She'd inherited it when he died a few years back. Jim kept the curtains closed. They had as little to do with their neighbors as possible. Couple months back a few of the kids who belonged to a houseboat down the way laughed at Ella. Saw her face and laughed at her. She stayed in the houseboat bed for four days. Kept the place totally dark. Wouldn't eat. Wouldn't even talk. Just kept herself unconscious with sleeping pills. Finally, he forced her to take a shower and eat the oatmeal and toast and strawberry jam he'd fixed for her. She couldn't take it when people laughed at her. Unlike Jim, Ella had never had any practice at being ugly, at being the outsider. Indeed, she'd always been the beauty. Cheerleader. Homecoming queen at Regis. Prime U of Iowa heartbreaker. Two rich husbands, both of whom had begged her to stay. And then a year-and-a-half ago when her rich friend (and possible husband #3) had been all coked up and accidentally smashed his big-ass Caddy convertible into a bridge abutment north of Iowa City, her life changed. How it changed. He'd died instantly. The seat belt had saved her life but hadn't done anything for her face. She'd gone through the windshield. Nearly a thousand stitches in her head and face. You ever see anybody with a thousand stitches in her head and face? We're talking your basic Frankenstein's monster here. The face now a series of slightly puffy sewn pockets, angled scars, red remnants of stitching. Snickers from little kids. Gasps from adults. She stayed in bed a lot. A *lot*. They were supposed to fly to Houston next month—there was a plastic surgeon there who'd developed some new techniques he thought might possible help her—but in the meantime Jim was still trying to get her to resume something like a normal life.

You're beautiful to me, Ella. That's all that matters.

You know, I don't even notice the scars any more, Ella. I really don't.

Don't worry, Ella. I'm paying them back. Every one of them.

These were the things he said to her over and over here in the course of their dark houseboat days.

He lived for that gentle drifting time after they made love and just held each other. Complete peace. The golden ship on the ancient sea, drifting toward Atlantis, just the two of them.

He wanted to be thinking of Atlantis right now—even awake he could sometimes conjure up that ship and that sea—but instead all he could think of was the missing gas can and that stack of *Cedar Rapids Gazettes* he'd kept about the fires he'd set. Somebody had gotten into the trunk of his car and taken them. He wondered who. He wondered why.

Four days ago, it had been. Opened the trunk to put some groceries in and—gone. He hadn't told Ella, of course. She didn't need any more grief. It was up to him to find out what was going on here. But how to start? Who to suspect?

He wanted to be one of them, one of the children running along the dock outside, laughing and having a good time. He wanted that for Ella, too. God, if only this Houston surgeon could do what he said he could do.

He eased himself off the bed, not wanting to wake her. He had a lot to do tonight. Time to visit the fourth and final dance club. Now, he'd have to buy a new can and fill it with gasoline. He'd also have to scope the place out. There were sure to be extra cops posted around clubs these days. He

30

might even have to wait a few days until the story faded from the headlines. He'd just have to see.

5

Matt, Jim's older brother said, "It was pretty funny to us —to me and Mom and Dad, I mean—for a while anyway. We lived in this real bad part of town and this really beautiful little girl named Ella Casey moved in down the street and Jim —he and Ella were both in sixth grade at the time—it changed his whole life. He was obsessed with her right from the start. And he didn't care who knew it, either. I mean, you know how boys don't like you to know that they've got a crush on somebody? He'd come right out and tell you. I can still hear him sitting in the kitchen with Mom after school, talking about all his plans for when he and Ella got married. Mom tried to help him with it—tried to make him see that she was just too, you know, beautiful for him, I mean, Jim isn't a handsome guy, I got the looks and he got the brains our Dad always said—but he didn't listen. He got this paper route and he spent all the money he earned from it on Ella. He was always buying her stuff. She'd take the stuff but she'd never go to a movie with him or go for a walk with him or anything. She was so beautiful, she's in ninth grade and she's got senior boys literally fighting over her. She was the fucking trophy, man. She was the trophy. And Jim was always there for her. Always. She'd invite him over when she was depressed or didn't know which boyfriend to choose or had some errand she needed run. And, man, he'd do whatever she wanted. He was like her shrink and her servant rolled into one. We thought maybe once he got out of high school, maybe one of them would go away to college. But Jim stayed here and went to the community college and she stayed in town and married this rich kid two days after she got out of high school. Eloped, because the kid's parents were against it. (Grinning) They were part of the Cedar Rapids jet set, you know what I'm saying?, and they just didn't want their very special little boy laying it to white trash every night. All the time they were married, poor Jim was her confidante. She was always calling him, crying and bitching about how unhappy she was. He got so caught up in her problems, he dropped out of school. He lived at home so all he'd have to have was a part-time job. He wanted to be there when Ella needed him. Finally, Ella couldn't handle the rich boy's family any more, so she divorced him and got a very nice settlement out of it.

"That's when she first started hitting the bars and the clubs. She'd never really done that before. Hadn't had to. But she was mid-twenties now and starting to slip, looks-wise, just a little. Still very, very sexy, but not the new kid on the block any more, either. She becomes the queen of the local clubs. Guys literally line up along the bar to talk to her. Only the best clubs, only the best guys, young lawyers and young docs and young investment bankers, guys like that.

"She ends up finding hubby number two in a club. Advertising guy who'd just sold his agency to a bigger shop out of Chicago. Plenty of cash and recently divorced. Mid-forties. Real fading ass-bandit type. But with pretensions. Guys like him used to get involved in charities so they could show everybody how cool they were. This decade, they dabble in the so-called arts. Local art museum board. Symphony board. Reading endowments for the underprivileged. Previous wife had been big in the Junior League so he's connected that way, too. And our little Ella is really taken in by all this. She thinks it's very sophisticated and elegant and all. She asks Jim—she's told her husband that Jim is gay, you know how a lot of women have male gay friends, and this fits right in with hubby's image of himself, the local *New Yorker*-type is how he sees himself, tells him Jim's gay even though he's not because this is the easiest way to explain the friend-ship—she asks Jim to start giving her some background on all the great painters and composers and like that. And he does, of course. And that's how things go for a few years until she starts having this thing with this college kid who buses dishes out at the club. Everybody in the club knows this is hap-pening except her husband. She's one of those women who doesn't hit thirty well. The rich ones head to the plastic sur-geons; the poor ones just have affairs. Ella does both. And then the new husband finds out and dumps her. He's cheated on every woman he's ever known but the one time he's the cheatee, his ego absolutely can't handle it. He gives her a lot of money on the condition that she gets out of his life immedi-ately, which she does. But she's already sick of the college boy, even though he's real serious about her.

"She's kind of in a panic, actually. Needs reassurance. This is the first time she ever lets Jim sleep with her. He told me about it, said she was having her period and everything, but he didn't care, even had oral sex with her, told her he wanted their blood to 'commingle.' Of course, he had to explain to her what 'commingle' meant but that was all right because she said it was 'beautiful.' She went back to the clubs. Of course, by this time, there's a whole new raft of beauties younger than she is. She's still got men lined up along the bar but the lines aren't quite as long as they once were. She's thirty-one now. And there's one thing she can never be again—and that's new. And that's what clubs like these always want. The new band. The new girl. The new drink. You know what I'm saying?

"Then she does the dumbest thing she's ever done in her life, she falls in love with this bartender whose putting it to

33

every babe in the place. He's got lines of women around the block, including all the newest and the hottest. And she falls in love with him. He goes out with her a few times—hammers her like she's never been hammered in her life—but then he dumps her. She's not used to being treated like this. In *her* life, it's supposed to be the other way around. She panics. Getting dumped undermines her whole life. She has money, a nice house, she can have all the plastic surgery she wants—but she knows that her time has passed as babe-of-the-moment.

"She starts stalking the bartender. She calls him night and day, she e-mails him, sends him flowers and candy, even gives him a car—a frigging Firebird, if you can believe it—and two or three times, she breaks into his apartment while he's hammering some other babe in his bedroom. One night, he's so frustrated, he punches her, gives her a black eye. Another night, she literally attacks his date in this restaurant. Throws her down on the floor and starts kicking her like some home boy would. And the *coup de grace*. She hides in his car, the car she bought him and he was asshole enough to accept, and at gunpoint forces him to take her for a long drive. She is very, very drunk. They drive around and around and she tells him all these plans she's got for when they get married. The first thing she wants with him, she says, is children. One boy, one girl. She's got access to enough cash to set him up in his own bar. An upscale one. No more club bullshit working for bosses who deal coke out their back door. And all of a sudden, he starts laughing at her. Which is not a good idea, somebody has a gun on you the way she does. By this time, they're up in the red clay cliffs. And she grabs the wheel from him and stomps her foot on his on the gas pedal and they go shooting right off the cliff. And we're talking a forty foot fall to the road below. He dies, her face is totally destroyed.

"Six, seven plastic surgeries in three years and there's not much improvement. The last one, though, she kind of convinces herself that she's looking better. And that's when she starts going back to the club scene. And it's a catastrophe. I only saw her once but she looked like a monster in a bad sci-fi flick. I mean, a $1.98 monster. But this monster is for real. People are so repelled by her, they don't even laugh at first (she tells Jim all this later on), they just shy back from her like she's got something contagious. Or she's like an omen that's going to bring them bad luck or something. Anyway, every place she goes, they just stare at her. The waitresses come over and they kind of smirk at her. And then people start getting mean. All the hotshots start asking her to dance. And some chick comes up and asks her what kind of makeup she's wearing. Not even the people she used to think of as friends want anything to do with her. She was a pretty ruthless little bitch when she was young and beautiful, and they're not all that sad to see her cut up this way. And every night, she goes up to her nice fancy lonely house and tells all this to Jim, who is by this time sort of her live-in shrink. And Jim is so pissed by what she's telling him—how she was treated in these clubs—that he starts setting the places on fire, the clubs I mean. For her, that's why he's doing it. For her. Because he wants her to know how much he loves her, how much he's willing to protect her. Because he knows that she'll marry him now. Ever since he was a kid, that was all he wanted. For her to marry him. And now it's finally going to happen."

6

Wind rattled the warped wood-framed windows. The linoleum was so old it was worn to floor in several places. The one big room smelled of cigarettes and Aqua Velva and whiskey, and a bathroom smelled of hair tonic and toilet bowl cleaner. There were doilies on the ragged armchair and the wobbly end tables and even on top of the bulky table model TV that dated from the sixties. The windows were so dirty you could barely see outside. If you listened carefully, you could hear the spectral echoes of all the lonely radio music that had been played in this shabby for-rent room down the decades, Bing Crosby in the Thirties and Frank Sinatra in the Forties and Elvis in The Fifties, and God only knew what else since then. A lot of animals crawl away to die in hidden shadowy places; this was a hidden shadowy place for humans.

"It's only $150 a month is why he lives here," Matt Shea said.

"They should pay him," I said.

"Yeah, it is pretty grim."

We'd spent three hours trying to find he and Ella. No luck. The times we'd called the landlady, she'd said he wasn't home. I finally said we should check out his apartment anyway. Shea agreed and here we were.

"We need to go to the police," I said.

"I know." He made a sour face. "This gets out, I'm going to have a hell of a time holding on to some of my clients. You don't want your lawyer having a god damned whacko for a brother."

He didn't seem unduly concerned about the people who'd died, or what fate awaited his brother.

He said, as if reading my mind, "I know I sound pretty selfish. But I came from the west side. I just don't want to see it all go to hell."

I started looking through the faded bureau. The mirror atop it was yellow. There were ghosts trapped in the mirror. You could sense them, dozens, maybe scores, of working men and women who died out their time in this room, staring at their fading lives in this mirror.

There was a bundle of photographs inside a manila envelope. There were maybe thirty pictures and every one of them was of the same person. Ella at ten, Ella at fifteen, Ella at twenty and so on. She was a true beauty, all right. Her smile could jar your teeth loose and give you a concussion. She was innocence and guile in equal measure, and she probably couldn't tell the difference between the two, and neither could you, not that you gave a damn anyway, she was trophy blond, eternal blonde, slender and supple goddess blonde, with just enough sorrow in the blue blue eyes to give her an air of fetching mystery, not ever completely knowable or possessable, this Ella girl and Ella woman, not ever.

I found it significant that there were no photos of them together. Ella was always alone. Beautiful and alone. The stuff of myth.

"Maybe he left town," Shea said.

"Maybe."

"She's got plenty of money. They could go anywhere."

"He isn't finished yet."

"Finished with what?"

I showed him the piece of Yellow Pages I'd just found in the bottom drawer. It had been ripped out, jagged. Under **DANCE CLUBS**, there were six names. He'd crossed off four of them.

"Looks like three to go," I said.

"That crazy son-of-a-bitch."

"We need to find him fast."

Then I saw the edge of another photo sticking out from beneath a sack of cheap white socks that were still in their plastic bagging.

"You find something else?" Shea said, as I stooped over.

"Uh-huh."

I snatched the photo and stared at it. "He a fisherman?"

"No way. Why?"

"He's got a photo of the marina here."

He took the photo from me. "Hey, I forgot about her houseboat."

"Ella's?"

"Yeah."

"Big-ass houseboat. Really fancy. Out at the Ellis marina."

"Sounds like it'd be worth checking out," I said.

"Yeah," he said. "It does."

7

Ellis Park was the place to go to see summer girls. At least it used to be when I'd visit my Cedar Rapids cousins back in the sixties and early seventies. The girls came in all colors and shapes and sizes and they were probably just as afraid of you as you were of them but their fear was more discreet than ours, and they passed by on bare sweet grass-flecked feet and tire-thrumming ten speed bikes and in the backs of shiny fine convertibles and on the rear ends of motorcycles driven by boys with biceps like softballs.

The summer girls were long gone now. Autumn was on the land, and on the water too, and the bobbing boats, mostly cabin-style or house boats, looked lonely in the dusk and the first faint light of winter stars. Here and there you saw cabin lights. In the summer they would have been welcoming and beacon bright but now there was something faded and desperate about them.

We pulled up on the ridge above the marina. Matt said, "I want to go down there alone first." Wimmers had been pulled on an emergency case, a bank robbery.

"The one you pointed out, there aren't any lights on."

"She doesn't want any lights on. Ever. Her face. He told me that. She gets pissed when he turns lights on." He shook his head. "All this shit comes out at the trial, I'm fucking dead meat. My father-in-law's a wheel at the country club. They're gonna be all over his ass."

"Maybe you should concentrate on your brother right now."

He glared at me. "Oh, I'm concentrating on him, all right. He's some psycho and he's going to destroy everything I built for myself in this town. So don't fucking tell me about concentration, all right, Payne?"

He got out of the car and then ducked his head back in. "If he's down there, I'll bring him back. You got any handcuffs or anything like that?"

"No."

"Great," he said. "Fucking great."

8

Every so often, Jim'd realize the significance of the moment. How long he'd loved her. How long she'd been denied him. And now, how free she was with him.

Lying in the big double bed on the house boat. In the darkness so she didn't feel bad about her face. Right next to her in that silk sleeping gown of hers. God her body. Such a perfect body. No reason for her to feel bad about her face when she had a body like that. No reason for her to feel bad about her face when he loved her so much. And someday, she'd *understand* that. That her face didn't matter as long he was there to protect her and comfort her.

Slight sway of boat, lying there; slight wind-cry outside in the night sky.

39

He worked himself against her spoon-fashion; a perfect match. Her sleeping. Careful not to wake her.

And then he heard it.

Somebody on the wooden walk of the marina. Footsteps coming this way.

Somebody.

He reached down to the floor where he kept the gun.

Somebody coming.

She'd argued with him about the gun at first. Guns scaring her. Guns going off when you didn't want them to and accidentally killing people. A gun was something only bad people owned. (Forgetting that she'd pulled a gun on the loverboy bartender.)

Now, he was glad he'd talked her into letting him keep it.

9

By the time Matt Shea reached the dock, he was lost in the dusk. Only as he passed lighted boats did I get a glimpse of his silhouette.

I wanted to be somewhere else. In a nice restaurant with a nice lady. Or in my Cedar Rapids apartment with my cats reading a book and dozing off under the lamp.

But not here with Matt Shea and all his country club concerns, and his sad crazed brother, and the once beautiful Ella. Sometimes, it's fun, the pursuit; but sometimes it's just sad, you learn something (or are reminded of something) you'd just as soon *not* know—the knowing changing you in some inalterable way—and then you wish you drove a cab or bagged up people's groceries.

He was gone fifteen minutes before I started to think about going down there.

All sorts of possibilities presented themselves. I'd kept the window rolled halfway down so I could hear shouts or screams. The marina was settling in for the night. A few cars wheeled into the parking lot. Men and women with liquor bottles tucked under their arms trekked from cars to boats. They laughed a lot and the laughter seemed wrong, even profane, given the moment, crazy Jim and scarred-up Ella. I waited another few minutes and then went down there.

The board walkway pitched beneath my feet. I could glimpse people behind houseboat curtains. They were searching for summer, even if it was only the memory of summer their boats offered them.

Ella's boat was three slips away from its nearest companion. This gave it a privacy the others lacked. No lights as I approached, no sound except the soft slap of water, and the tangle of night birds in the tangle of autumn trees.

I jumped aboard and went to the door. Locked. I walked to the window to the left of the curtain. The curtains were pulled tight. I listened carefully. Nothing.

And then I heard the sobbing. Male sobbing. Throaty and uncomfortable, as if the man didn't *know* how to sob, hadn't had sufficient practice.

I went to the door. Tried the knob again. Useless. "Matt? Are you in there?"

The sobbing. Barely audible.

I got out the burglary tools I keep in my pocket most of the time. I went in and clipped a light on.

Smell of blood and feces. And something even fouler. He brought it with him when he staggered up off the chair and fell into my arms. Matt Shea.

The knife was still in his chest. Just to the right of his heart. A long, pearl-handled switchblade. The sobs were his. "This is really going to look like shit in the papers tomorrow." All this, and his primary concern was still his rep with the country club boys. "Son-of-a-bitch stabbed me. His own brother."

I half-carried him back to the chair he'd been in and sat him down. There might still be time for an ambulance. I went to the phone and dialed 911.

The boat was laid out with bunks on both sides, a tiny kitchen, and a living room arrangement dominating the center of the room. The couch had been opened up to become a bed and now there were two people in it. One of them was alive. That was Jim Shea. The other was dead, six, seven days into death judging by what I could see of the lividity and rigor mortis. The body was bloated and badly discolored. There were flies and maggots, too. The facial flesh itself had separated and spoiled but even so you could still see the scarring. Jim Shea didn't seem to notice any of this. He wore a black T-shirt and chinos. He lay up against her, an arm wrapped around her hip with great proprietary fondness. She was his woman, the woman he'd dreamt of most of his life, and he wasn't going to let go of her even now. He probably didn't even know she'd been dead for nearly a week. Or maybe he didn't care. She wore a white blouse and a dark skirt. No blanket covered them. There was a bullet wound in her right temple. I was going to say something to him but then I looked at his eyes and saw that it was no use. Certain mad saints had eyes like his, and visionaries, and men who believe that God told them to go down to the local school and open fire on the children on the playground.

The note was still on the small dining table. Simple enough. She couldn't handle it and killed herself. But he'd kept right on taking care of her, killing those who had made fun of her at the clubs.

"I work my ass off and make something of my life and this is what I fucking get for it," Matt Shea said somewhere behind me.

10

After the DA decided to go with a plea bargain and a reduced sentence—Jim Shea's defense attorney deciding to drop the insanity defense even though Jim was clearly insane —I got a call from Matt Shea thanking me for everything. He said things hadn't gone so badly for him, after all. In fact, ironically, some of the members feeling badly for him, he'd been nominated to sit on the board of the country club. First time a west sider had ever been nominated.

Then he said, "You hear about Jim?"

"No."

"Killed himself."

He was so calm, I thought he might be talking about some other Jim. "Your brother?"

"Yeah. Started squirreling socks away in jail. Made a noose for himself." Pause. "I know you think I'm a callous bastard, Payne. But it's better for everybody."

"He belonged in a psychiatric hospital."

"You know what that fucking trial would've done to me? All those headlines day after day? They wouldn't've done my mother any good, either, believe me."

"That's touching, you caring about your mother and all."

"Believe it or not, Payne, I do. And Jim was never anything but a burden to her. His whole life. If he'd lived, she would've had to go up to the penitentiary and see him every month."

"You wouldn't have?"

"Sure, sometimes. When I had the time, I mean. But prisons spook me. Like hospitals. Or graveyards. I just think it's bad luck to be anywhere around them. Well, I just thought I'd catch you up on some things. You get my check by the way?"

"Very generous. I appreciate it."

"You helped me, Payne, and I appreciate it. Well, listen, gotta run."

My first thought was to have one of those dramatic little moments you see in bad movies and tear his check up into a thousand pieces. Moral outrage.

But then I realized that I badly needed the money, the old cash flow not being so hot lately.

I went down and deposited it right away. Just the way Matt Shea would have.

A Girl Like You

And hearts that we broke long ago/

Have long been breaking others.—W. H. Auden

He knew they were in trouble and he couldn't eat. He knew they were in trouble and he couldn't sleep. He knew they were in trouble and he couldn't concentrate.

Not on anything except his girl Nora.

His name was Peter Wyeth and he was eighteen, all ready to enter the state university this fall, and he'd met her two-and-a-half-months ago at a kegger on graduation night. He'd been pretty bombed, so bombed in fact that she'd driven him home in the new Firebird his folks had bought him for graduation.

That first night, she hadn't seemed like so much. Or maybe it was that he'd been so bombed he didn't realize just how much she really was. The truth was, Peter pretty much took girls for granted. He could afford to. He had the Wyeth look. There was some Dartmouth about the Wyeth boys, even though they'd lived all their lives here in small-town Iowa; and something Smith about the Wyeth girls. Between them, they broke a lot of hearts hereabouts, and if they didn't seem to take any particular pleasure in it, still they didn't seem to care much either.

Nora Caine was different somehow.

He'd never seen or heard of her before the night of the kegger. But he asked about her a lot the next day. Somebody said that they thought she was from one of those little towns near the point where Iowa and Wisconsin faced each other across the Mississippi. Visiting somebody here. It was all vague.

He ran into her that night at Charlie's, which was the sports bar on the highway where you could drink if you had a fake ID. Or if you were a Wyeth. She was dancing with some guy he recognized as a university frosh football player, something Peter himself had planned to be until he'd damaged his knee in a game against Des Moines.

He didn't like it. That was the first thing he noticed. And he realized instantly that he'd never felt this particular feeling before. Jealousy. He didn't even know this girl and yet he was jealous that she was dancing with somebody else. What the hell was that all about? Wyeths didn't get jealous; they didn't need to.

He watched her for the next hour. If she was teasing him, she was doing it subtly. Except for a few glances, she didn't seem aware of him at all. She just kept dancing with the frosh. By this time, Peter's friends were there and they were standing all around him telling him just how beautiful Nora Caine was. As if he needed to be told. What most fascinated him about her physically was a certain . . . timelessness . . . about her. Her hair style wasn't quite contemporary. Her clothes hinted at another era. Even her dance steps seemed a little dated. And yet she bedazzled, fascinated, imprisoned him.

Nora Caine.

She left that night with the frosh.

Peter spent a sleepless night—the first of many, as things

would turn out—and knew just what he'd do at first light. He'd go looking for her. Somebody had to know who she was, where she lived, what she was doing here in town.

He met her that afternoon. She was sitting along the peaceful river, a sleek black raven sitting next to her, as if it was keeping guard. Her apartment was only a block from here. The landlady, impressed that she was talking to young Wyeth, told him everything she knew about Nora. Girl was here for a few weeks settling some kind of family matters with an attorney. The frosh football player a constant visitor. Nora listening to classical music (played low), given to long walks along the river (always alone), and painting lovely pictures of days gone by.

"You remember me?"

She looked up. "Sure."

"Thanks for driving me home the other night. How'd you get home?"

"Walked."

"You could've taken a cab and just told them to put it on my father's account."

"He must be an important man."

"He is." Then: "Mind if I sit down?"

"I sort of have a boyfriend."

"The football player?"

"Yes." She smiled and he was cut in half so profound was the effect of her smile on him. He wanted to cry in both joy and sorrow, joy for her smile, sorrow for her words. He felt scared, and wondered if he might be losing his mind. He'd been drinking too much beer lately, that was for sure. "The funny thing is, I don't even like sports."

"I'd like to go out with you sometime."

"I guess I'm just not sure how things're going to go with Brad. So I really can't make any dates."

47

A few weeks later—well into outrageous green suffocating summer now—Peter heard that Brad took a bad spill on his motorcycle. Real bad. He'd be in University hospital for several months.

He'd tried to distract himself with the wildest girls he could find. He had a lot of giggles and a lot of sex and a lot of brewskis and yet he was still soul-empty. He'd never felt like this. Empty this way. Empty and scared and lonely and jealous. What the hell was it about Nora anyway? Sure, she was beautiful but so were most of his girls. Sure, she was winsome and sweet but so were some of the girls he'd dated seriously. Sure, she was—And then he realized what it was. He couldn't have her. That was what was so special about her. If she'd ever just give in to him the way the other girls did . . . he wouldn't want her.

She was just playing games like all the other girls (or so he'd always imagined they were playing games anyway) and he was—for the first time—losing.

He did a very irrational thing one rainy night. He parked in the alley behind her apartment house and watched as she left the house. He climbed the fire escape along the back and broke into her room and there he saw her paintings. They were everywhere, leaning against the walls, set in chairs, standing on one of the three easels. As silver rain eeled down the windows, he stood in the lightning-flashes of the night and escaped into the various worlds she had painted. They looked like magazine cover illustrations from every decade in this century—the doughboys of World War I, the hollow-eyed farmers of the Depression, the dogfaces of World War II, a young girl with a 1950s hula hoop, an anti-Vietnam hippie protester, a stockbroker on the floor, Times Square the first night of the new century. There was a reality to the illustrations that gave him a dizzy feeling, as if they were drawing him into the world they represented. He'd have to give up smoking so much pot, too. It obviously wasn't doing him any good.

Then she came home, carrying a small damp sack of groceries, her red hair bejeweled with raindrops. The funny thing was she didn't even ask him why he was here. She just set down the groceries and came to him.

Not long after that, a local newspaper editor, Paul Sheridan, came up on the street to him and said, "I see you know Nora Caine. She's going to teach you a lot." As always, the white-haired, ruddy-cheeked Sheridan smelled of liquor. He was in his sixties. As a young man, he'd written a novel that had sold very well. But that was the end of his literary career. He could never seem to find a suitable subject for a second novel. His wife and daughter had died in a fire some time ago. He had inherited the newspaper from his father and ran it until his drinking caused him to bring in his cousin, who ran the paper and did a better job than Paul ever had. Now Paul wrote some editorials, some reviews of books nobody in a town like this would ever read, and did pieces on town history, at which he excelled. There was always talk that somebody should collect these pieces that stretched back now some twenty-five years but as yet nobody had. Sheridan said: "If you're strong, Peter, you'll be the better man for it."

What the hell was Sheridan muttering about? How did he even know that Peter knew Nora? And how the hell did anybody Sheridan's age know Nora?

It was two weeks before she'd let Peter sleep with her. He was crazy by then. He was so caught up in her, he found himself thinking unimaginable things: he wouldn't go to college, he'd get a job so they could get married. And they'd have a kid. He didn't want to lose her and he lived in constant terror that he would. But if they had a kid . . . When he was away from her, he was miserable. His parents took to giving him long confused looks. He no longer returned the calls of his buddies—they seemed childish to him now. Nora was the one lone true reality. He would not wash his hands sometimes for long periods; he wanted to retain their intimacy. He learned things about women—about fears and appetites and nuances. And he learned about heartbreak. The times they'd argue, he was devastated when he realized that someday she might well leave him.

And so it went all summer.

He took her home. His parents did not care for her. "Sort of . . . aloof" his mother said. "What's wrong with Tom Bolan's daughter? She's a lot better looking than this Nora and she's certainly got a nicer pair of melons" his father said. To which his mother predictably replied, "Oh, Lloyd, you and your melons. Good Lord."

They avoided the old places he used to go. He didn't want to share her.

There was no intimacy they did not know, sexual, mental, spiritual. She even got him to go to some lectures at the University on Buddhism and he found himself not enraptured (as she seemed to be) but at least genuinely interested in the topic and the discussion that followed.

He would lay his hand on her stomach and dream of the kid they'd have. He'd see toddlers on the street and try to imagine what it'd be like to have one of his own. And you know what, he thought it would be kinda cool, actually. It really would be.

And then, this one morning, she was gone.

Her landlady told him that a cab had shown up right at nine o'clock this morning and taken her and her two bags (they later found that she'd shipped all her canvases and art supplies separately) and that she was gone. She said to tell Peter goodbye for her.

He'd known they were in some sort of trouble these past couple of weeks—something she wouldn't discuss—but now it had all come crashing down.

A cab had picked her up. Swept her away. Points unknown.

Tell Peter goodbye for me.

He had enemies. The whole Wyeth family did. Whenever anything bad happened to one of the Wyeths the collective town put on a forlorn face of course (hypocrisy not being limited to Madison Avenue cocktail parties) and then proceeded to chuckle when the camera was off them.

A fine handsome boy, they said, too bad.

He wasn't a fine boy, though, and everybody knew it. He had treated some people terribly. Girls especially. Get them all worked up and tell them lots of lies and then sleep with them till a kind of predatory spell came over him and he was stalking new blood once again. There had been two abortions; a girl who'd sunk into so low a depression that she had to stay in a hospital for a time; and innumerable standard-issue broken hearts. He was no kinder to males. Boys who amused him got to warm themselves in the great presence of a Wyeth; but when they amused him no longer—or held strong opinions with which he disagreed or hinted that maybe his family wasn't all that it claimed to be—they were banished forever from the golden kingdom.

So who could argue that the bereaved, angry, sullen, despondent, boy who had been dumped by a passing-through girl . . . who could argue that he didn't deserve it?

His mother suggested a vacation. She had family in New Hampshire.

His father suggested Uncle Don in Wyoming. He broke broncos; maybe he could break Peter who was embarrassing to be around these days. By God, and over a girl too.

He stayed in town. He drank and he slept off the drink and then he drank some more. He was arrested twice for speeding, fortunately when he was sober. And—back with his friends again—he was also fined for various kinds of childish mischief, not least of which was spray painting the F word on a police car.

Autumn came; early autumn, dusky ducks dark against the cold mauve melancholy prairie sky, his friends all gone off to college, and Peter more alone than he'd ever been.

His father said he needed to get a job if he wasn't going to the university.

His mother said maybe he needed to see a psychologist.

He was forced, for friendship, to hang out with boys he'd always avoided before. Not from the right social class. Not bright or hip or aware. Factory kids or mall kids, the former sooty when they left the mill at three every afternoon; the latter dressed in the cheap suits they wore to sell appliances or tires or cheap suits. And yet, after an initial period of feeling superior, he found that these kids weren't really much different from his other friends. All the same fears and hopes. And he found himself actually liking most of them. Understanding them in a way he would have thought impossible.

There was just one thing they couldn't do: they couldn't save him from his grief. They couldn't save him and booze couldn't save him and pot couldn't save him and speed couldn't save him and driving fast couldn't save him and fucking his brains out and sobbing couldn't save him and puking couldn't save him and masturbating couldn't save him and hitting people couldn't save him and praying couldn't save him. Not even sleep could save him, for always in sleep came Nora. Nora Nora Nora. Nothing could save him.

And then the night—his folks at the country club—he couldn't handle it any more. Any of it. He lay on his bed with his grandfather's straight razor and cut his wrists. He was all drunked up and crying and scared shitless but somehow he found the nerve to do it. Just at the last minute, blood starting to cover his hands now, he rolled over on the bed to call 911 but then he dropped the receiver. Too weak. And then he went to sleep . . .

He woke up near dawn in a very white room. Streaks of dawn in the window. The hospital just coming awake. Rattle of breakfast carts; squeak of nurses' shoes. And his folks peering down at him and smiling and a young woman doctor saying, "You're going to be fine, Peter. Just fine."

His mother wept and his father kept whispering, "You'll have to forgive your mother. She used to cry when you two would watch Lassie together," which actually struck Peter as funny.

"I'll never get over her," he said.

"You'll be back to breaking hearts in no time," his father said.

"She wasn't our kind anyway," his mother said. "I don't mean to be unkind, honey, but that's the truth."

"I still wish you'd give old Tom's daughter a go," his father said.

"Yeah, I know," Peter said. "Melons." He grinned. He was glad he wasn't dead. He felt young and old; totally sane and totally crazy; horny and absolutely monastic; drunk and sober.

He went home the next day. And stayed home. It was pretty embarrassing to go out. People looking at you. Whispering.

He watched Nick at Night a lot. Took him back to the days when he was six and seven. You have it knocked when you're six and seven and you don't even realize it. Being six and seven—no responsibilities, no hassles, no doom—is better than having a few billion in the bank. He stayed sober; he slept a lot; every once in awhile the sorrow would just overwhelm him and he'd see her right in front of him in some fantastical way, and hear her and feel her and smell her and taste her and he would be so balled-up in pain that not only would he want to be six or seven, he wanted to go all the way back to the womb.

March got all confused and came on like May. My God you just didn't know what to do with yourself on days like this. Disney had a hand in creating a day like this; he had to.

He started driving to town and parking and walking around. He always went mid-afternoon when everybody was still in school. He never would've thought he'd be so happy to see his old town again. He took particular notice of the trolly tracks and the hitching posts and the green Model-T you could see all dusty in Old Man Baumhofer's garage. He sat in the library and actually read some books, something he'd never wanted to do in his whole life.

But mostly he walked around. And thought thoughts he'd never thought before either. He'd see a squirrel and he'd wonder if there was some way to communicate with the little guy that human beings—in their presumptuousness and arrogance—just hadn't figured out yet. He saw flowers and stopped and really studied them and lovingly touched them and sniffed them. He saw infants in strollers being pushed by pretty young moms with that twenty-year-old just-bloomed beauty that flees so sadly and quickly; and saw the war memorials of three different conflicts and was proud to see how many times the name Wyeth was listed. He looked—for the first time in his life he really looked at things. And he loved what he saw; just loved it.

And one day when he was walking down by the deserted mill near the newspaper office, he saw Paul Sheridan just leaving and he went up to him and he said, "Awhile back you told me Nora was going to teach me things. And that if I was strong I'd be a better man for it."

For the first time, he looked past the drunken red face and the jowls and the white hair and saw Sheridan as he must have been at Peter's age. Handsome and tall, probably a little theatrical (he still was now), and possessed of a real warmth. Sheridan smiled: "I knew you'd look me up, kiddo. C'mon in the office. I want to show you something."

Except for a couple of pressmen in the back, the office was empty. Several computer stations stood silent, like eyes guarding against intruders.

Sheridan went over to his desk and pulled out a photo album. He carried it over to a nearby table and set it down. "You want coffee?"

"That sounds good."

"I'll get us some. You look through the album."

He looked through the album. Boy, did he. And wondered who the jokester was who'd gone to all this trouble.

Here were photographs—some recent, some tinted in turn-of-the-last-century-fashion—of Nora Caine in dozens of different poses, moods, outfits—and times. Her face never changed, though. She was Nora in the 1890s and she was Nora today. There could be no mistaking that.

Goosebumps; disbelief.

"Recognize her?" Sheridan said when he sat down. He pushed a cup of coffee Peter's way.

"Somebody sure went to a lot of trouble to fake all these photographs."

Sheridan smiled at him. "Now you know better than that. You're just afraid to admit it."

"Sure, they're real."

"But that's impossible."

"No, it's not. Not if you're an angel or a ghost or whatever the hell she is." He sipped some coffee. "She broke my heart back when I was your age. So bad I ended up in a mental hospital having electroshock treatments. No fun, let me tell you. Took me a long time to figure out what she did for me."

"You mean, did *to* you?"

"No; that's the point. You have to see her being with you for a positive thing rather than a negative one. I was a spoiled rich kid just like you. A real heartbreaker. Didn't know shit from shinola and didn't care to. All I wanted to do was have fun. And then she came along and crushed me—and turned me into a genuine human being. I hated her for at least ten years. Tried to find her. Hired private detectives. Everything. I wrote my novel about her. Only novel I had in me as things turned out. But I never would've read a book; or felt any compassion for poor people; or cared about spiritual things. I was an arrogant jerk and it took somebody like her to change me. It had to be painful or it wouldn't have worked. I was bitter and angry for a long time like I said but then eventually I saw what she'd done for me. And I thanked her for it. And loved her all the more. But in a different way now."

"You don't really believe she's some kind of ghost or something do you?"

"The photos are real, Peter. Took me thirty years to collect them. I went all over the Midwest collecting them. I'd show a photo to somebody in some little town and then they'd remember her or remember somebody who'd known her. And it was always the same story. Some arrogant young prick—rich or poor, black or white didn't matter—and he'd have his fling with her. And then she'd move on. And he'd be crushed. But he'd never be his arrogant old self again. Some of them couldn't handle it and they'd kill themselves. Some of them would just be bitter and drink themselves to death. But the strong ones—us, Peter, you and me—we learned the lessons she wanted us to. Just think of all the things we know now we didn't know before she met us."

The phone rang. He got up to get it. Peter noticed that he staggered a little.

He was on the phone for ten minutes. No big deal. Just a conversation with somebody about a sewer project. You didn't usually get big deals on some town newspapers like this one.

Peter just looked at the pictures. His entire being yearned for a simple touch of her. In her flapper outfit. Or her WW II Rosie-The-Riveter get-up. Or her hippie attire. Nora Nora Nora.

Sheridan came back from the phone. "I didn't expect you to believe me, Peter. I didn't believe it for a long time. Now I do." He looked at him for a time. "And someday you will, too. And you'll be grateful that she was in your life for that time." He grinned and you could see the boy in him suddenly. "She had some ass, didn't she?"

Peter laughed. "She sure did."

"I got to head over to the library, kiddo."

Sheridan said goodbye to the pressmen and then they headed out the door. The day was still almost oppressively beautiful.

"This is the world she wanted me to see, Peter. And I never would've appreciated it if I hadn't loved her."

They crossed the little bridge heading to the merchant

blocks. Sheridan started to turn right toward the library.

"The next woman you love, you'll know how to love. How to be tender with her. How to give yourself to her. I can't say that my life has been a great success, Peter. It hasn't been. But I loved my wife and daughter more than I ever could've if I hadn't met Nora. Maybe that's the most important thing she ever taught us, Peter." And with that, Sheridan waved goodbye.

Six years later his wife Faith gave birth to a girl. Peter asked if they might name her Nora. And Faith, understanding, smiled yes.

The Way It Used to Be

Private coon hunting. That's all the note said, the note passed three desks back in last hour study hall, that lazy hour when half the students dozed off.

When Boze Douglas opened the note and read the three words, he smiled. No doubt who'd sent the note. No doubt what it meant. No doubt.

Boze kept right on smiling.

He couldn't concentrate on his comic book any more. Boze was a master at laying a comic book inside a textbook and then pretending to be studying his ass off. He liked superheroes especially. In his own mind, he was a superhero. The fact that nobody else at Duncan County Consolidated saw him as a superhero only proved what lame bastards they were. Duncan County Consolidated was one of those country high schools where kids from five small towns went to school together. Farm kids, too. Lots and lots of farm kids. Kids who didn't know, kids who weren't cool, not the way Boze and his friend Gunner (a.k.a. Eugene) Preston were cool. Boze and Gunner were wearing nose rings and earrings long before anybody else at Duncan County Consolidated was. And they were way into heavy music and street drugs before most of the other kids, too. And they were tough. Even the big loping farm boys were smart enough to walk clear of Boze and Gunner. Most students—and teachers—considered them dangerous and, man, they loved that shit, people seeing them as dangerous. Absolutely loved it.

"He's gonna be surprised," Gunner said, lighting up a Camel as soon as they cleared the school door.

There was a big football game tonight and so part of the east parking lot was given over to last minute work on the float where the King and Queen would sit tonight. King and Queen, Boze thought. That was crap for little kids. King and Queen. In the distance, he could hear the marching band practicing in the field to the north of the large red brick school. He had to admit, reluctantly, that marching band music still gave him a little-kid thrill. He'd always liked parades. His father had always taken him to parades . . . At least when he was sober. But padre was long gone. Living over in Keokuk with wife number three, selling mobile homes. Now, marching band music—as much as it still secretly thrilled Boze—embarrassed him, too.

Then they were in Boze's five-year-old Firebird and driving fast. This was the best way for Boze to avoid thinking about things—thinking about long-gone Dad, thinking about all the bullshit his sixteen-year-old sister Angie had fallen into—driving fast. Not even drugs were as good as driving fast.

Farm fields in sunny October. Pumpkins and scarecrows and the green John Deere working the hills, preparing for spring planting. And that melancholy smoky smell down from the hills where the trees were on fire with colors so beautiful—reds and yellows and golds and ambers—that they were almost painful to see.

And Angie—little Angie, his own little sister—was going out with a black guy. He still couldn't believe it, though he knew it was absolutely true.

Boys could handle going to Cedar Rapids. There were a lot of temptations for farm kids in a town that size but boys knew how to stay away from them. Or if they couldn't handle them, it still wasn't so bad. They were boys, after all. A white boy and a black girl going out together, much as Boze was against such a thing, that was all right. No harm done. The boy wasn't likely to get all emotional with the black girl. But a white girl with a black boy . . . once you go black, you'll never go back? Wasn't that what he'd heard his old man say to a friend of his, laughing and winking, one beery night?

Boze drove a good ten miles out into the countryside. He hit 104 mph crossing the old Miller bridge. Even the horses and the cows and the sheep seemed to stand still and watch with awe as the Firebird blazed by. The radio was up all the way. Country music all the way. He used to listen to rock but now it was all fairies or coons. Now he was strictly country. On the way back to town, Gunner said, "You scared?"

"About what?"

"You know. Tonight."

Boze looked over at him. "No. But you are."

"Bullshit."

"Bullshit yourself, man. If you weren't scared, you wouldn't have brought it up."

"I just mean we could get caught there. You know, down there with all those black bastards."

"Yeah, we could. But we're not gonna. We're gonna do it and get the hell out of there." That was Gunner for you. Everybody thought he was like this really fearless dude. But he wasn't. He talked big and he had big ideas. But when it came to actually doing them, Boze was the one who always led the way. Gunner wouldn't have done anything if Boze didn't drag him along.

Boze dropped Gunner off. Gunner lived in a small housing development. Most of the people here worked in nearby Amana—factory jobs and good paying ones. New or at least newer cars in the drives now that the day shift was over. And new siding on a lot of the houses. Boze had always envied Gunner his industrious and sober old man. Gunner had it made here and didn't seem to know it. As he was getting out of the car, Gunner said, "I'm really not scared, man. I'm really not."

"Then you'll do it?"

"Fuckin' right." Trying to sound tough, hard. But Boze could see the fear in his eyes. This was a couple steps up the criminal ladder from the shoplifting and minor vandalism they were usually into. This was quite a ways up the criminal ladder, in fact.

"I'll pick you up at seven," Boze said.

"Cool," Gunner said, closing the door. Cool, Boze thought to himself as the Firebird squealed away from the curb. Sometimes Gunner was such a lame, he couldn't believe it.

Mom wasn't home yet. Sometimes Al at the restaurant, a slow afternoon, he'd let her off a little early and pay her for the whole day. Mom liked Al despite the fact that the old bastard was always putting the moves on her. He wasn't alone, of course, Al wasn't, Mom being a good-looking woman and lots of men hitting on her. But she said it was "sweet," a seventy-two-year-old guy hitting on a thirty-eight-year-old woman. Plus, it was the best waitressing job she'd ever had. Great tips and nice family-style restaurant. She'd burned out on butt-pinching truck stops and stingy-ass truck drivers.

On a sunny day like this one, the trailer park didn't look so bad. The dirt roads winding between the half mile of mobile homes were dry and not muddy; and fresh wash hanging on clotheslines looked white and clean; and even the battered trailers themselves—screens missing, some graffiti here and there, cracked windows taped up—looked reasonably clean and tidy, tiny strips of lawns covered with dirt roads.

When he got inside, he heard music coming from Angie's room. Rap music. He should have taken that as a sign for sure, last year when she'd started listening to that crap. White girls, at least not good white girls, didn't listen to blacks who couldn't (a) sing (b) write songs, or (c) look like anything but the street punks they were.

At least she'd cleaned up the house. Angie was the neat freak of the family, mostly because she had friends over a lot—she even had a couple of fairly rich friends from in town; she was a friendly and bright and popular girl, she was—and she hated it the way Mom and Boze always left ashtrays overflowing and half-drunk cans of beer and pop strewn everywhere. Not to mention magazines and newspapers and even the occasional half-eaten sandwich. Dad was a neat freak too, unlikely as that was. Angie had inherited the tendency from him.

He knocked on her door and then pushed in without waiting for her to answer.

"Damn you!" she cried when he burst in.

She was standing at her bureau mirror, combing her long, chestnut-colored hair. Her hair was her pride, as were the high proud breasts she'd sprouted last summer. She was dressed only in a white slip now. Despite the anger he felt—how the hell could she go out with a black guy, anyway?—he wished now he hadn't broken in like this. He looked uncomfortable seeing his fetching sister half-undressed this way. He wanted to think of her the way he used to . . . as a sweet little kid he was always very protective of. He'd even walked to school with her, to make sure she was all right, even though the other boys used to make fun of him. When it started to storm, he'd always panicked, searched frantically through the

63

trailer park until he had her inside and safe. And when she'd been sick with flu or a sore throat or something, he'd always brought her stupid little gifts, and tried to make her laugh so she'd feel better. And then she changed. Last year, it was. Maybe it was her breasts. Maybe her breasts had made her crazy or something. Suddenly, she resented all his fondness, all his protectiveness. How many times in the past year had she screamed at him. It's my life and I'll do what I damned well please! He always felt vaguely sick—even mysteriously fearful—when she screamed this. He felt deserted, more alone than he ever had in his life, even more alone than when Mom and Dad split up six years ago.

And now she was going out with a black guy.

"I'm really getting tired of this, Boze," she said. "You're supposed to knock."

He kept his eyes from her as much as he could. What he really wanted to do was say it. Say he knew about the black guy he had seen pulling away from the trailer here on two different occasions. Linn County plates. Cedar Rapids. Boze hadn't gotten all that good a look at him. But he didn't have to. The guy was black, wasn't he? Wasn't that enough?

But Boze didn't say it because if he did say it she'd run right to Mom and tell her everything, and Mom didn't need any more grief than she already had. It wasn't easy, holding the family together this way, let alone your daughter going out with a black guy. Obviously, there was no way Angie was going to tell Mom—I been going out with this black guy, Mom. And wouldn't Mom just love that? Mom knew a lot about men and men problems. She'd dated a lot of different guys since Dad left. She knew all the ways a woman could get screwed up over a man. And that certainly included dating someone not of your own race. Mom would tear Angie a new one if she ever found out about the black guy.

Boze decided to be coy. "Where you going tonight?"

"Out."

"I know 'out.' I mean where?"

She looked angry a moment and then she smiled sentimentally at him in the mirror. She was putting on bright red lipstick. Blood red. The color she'd be if the black guy ever cut her up with his switchblade. Boze knew all about black guys and their knives. "I'm not six years old any more, Boze. You don't have to protect me."

"I have to protect you more than ever," he said gently.

She turned and came over to him. He tried not to look at her breasts loose beneath her white silk slip. No bra. She kissed him. "I'm sorry I got so mad a minute ago."

"It's all right."

"No, it isn't." She leaned forward and kissed him on the cheek. She smelled sweetly of perfume. It was like she wasn't his sister at all. She was as full of wiles as any other girl, now. He felt sad for some reason. He wanted her to be six or seven or eight again, and have her tiny hand in his, and be helping her. He'd liked to help her. It made him feel important somehow. He hadn't felt important much lately at all. "And since you asked," she said, withdrawing, going back to the mirror and the comb and her hair, "I'm going to Cedar Rapids with Donna and Heather."

"You should stay away from that place."

She watched him coolly in the mirror. "So should you. You're the one who got in trouble there. Not me." The edge was back in her voice now.

He was about to defend himself—pointing out that all he got charged with that time was underage drinking and public intoxication, not exactly murder one—when the front door opened and Mom said, "Hi, kids!"

It was always good to hear her voice. "Hi!" they both said back to her.

Mom set the sack of groceries on the table and then walked back to the bedroom. "How do vegetable burgers and a salad sound for tonight?"

She smelled of perfume, too, and then Boze realized that Angie was wearing Mom's perfume. Mom was short, slender, with long, dark hair and turquoise eyes. She usually wore jeans and crisp white blouses and argyle socks and a pair of comfortable walking shoes. The saddest he'd ever seen her was when Dad gave her that black eye that time. Usually when he beat her up, you couldn't see anything. But the black eye had really embarrassed her. That had been near the end of the marriage.

Mom said, "I take it you're both going out tonight?"

Boze smiled. "No, I thought I'd stay home and do a little knitting."

Mom loved it when he joked with her. When her marriage had been good, before Dad really got going on the booze, Dad had kidded around a lot with her, too. "Oh, you," she said, poking Boze in the ribs. But she looked tired, despite the smile and the kidding, and sometimes he worried about her, how tired and suddenly old she could look. A great sorrow overcame him at such times and all he could think of was funeral homes when he was little, the mysterious adult ritual of putting the dead to rest, the choking-sweet smell of flowers and the whiskey-breath of the working men as they bent down to kiss their little nephews and nieces and the smell of his mother's Kleenex damp with Hail Mary tears when she'd knelt next to the coffin.

Half an hour later, they ate. The burgers were delicious. Part of the time Boze looked out the window. Dusk was falling and it was beautiful, the sky gorgeous golds and salmon pinks and rich purples behind a few full thunderheads. Dusk made Boze sad, too, but it was a good sad somehow, not a bad sad like with Angie or Mom or Dad or Molly Cantrell when he was in love with her last year. That was just one more crazy thing in an already crazy world; how there could be good sails and bad sails. But it wasn't the kind of thing you ever talked about because people would think you were crazy.

Mom said, "You remember you're supposed to be home by eleven tonight?"

"Oh, Mom," Angie said. "That's not fair."

"It certainly is fair, Angie," Mom said. "You were late last Friday night by an hour, so tonight I'm taking an hour off the time you're supposed to be in."

"But eleven o'clock. Nobody else has to come in by eleven o'clock."

"I'm sorry, Angie. But that's the way it's got to be."

Boze lifted weights for twenty minutes while he watched The Nashville Channel (say what you want, Dwight Yoakam was still the coolest of all the male country singers) and then he took a shower and then he got dressed for the night. He put change and a ten-dollar bill in his right pocket (Mom always gave him a ten-dollar bill on Friday) and his twelve-inch switchblade in his left pocket. Anything over twelve inches, the cops could bust your ass for carrying an illegal weapon. Then he got down on his haunches and opened the bottom drawer. There was a small grey metal lockbox in there. He opened it up. The .38 snub nose pistol looked as imposing as ever. Mom'd kick his ass if she ever found out he had it. Same way she'd kick Angie's ass if she ever found out Angie was going out with the black guy.

He loaded the .38 and stuffed it down the front of his pants. Down in black town, man, you couldn't have enough weapons. Not on a Friday night, you couldn't.

Angie was in the living room still arguing with Mom about eleven o'clock. Boze gave Mom a kiss on the cheek. Angie looked beautiful, purple blouse, hip-hugger slacks, high heels. Her sexuality was overwhelming. He imagined black hands on that white flesh. The image sickened him.

"You've got hours, too, Boze, don't forget," Mom said. "Twelve o'clock."

Boze grinned. "You make a great boot camp instructor, I ever tell you that?"

Mom grinned back. "Many times."

Then Boze was out of there. In the car. Driving fast on empty country roads just as the half-moon was rising above the cornfields and all the little farmhouses whose lights seemed curiously lonely in the gloom. Dwight Yoakam was singing his ass off. Boze had half an hour by himself driving this way—a can of beer from the trunk in one hand, a cigarette in the other—just driving, driving fast all by himself before he had to pick up Gunner.

There was a certain part of the Interstate when you were coming into Cedar Rapids . . . if you looked fast enough, it was like coming into a really big city . . . the way three or four tall buildings were silhouetted against the moon . . . and the way the neon chain of lights seemed to stretch forever into the prairie night and the way crosstown traffic was almost bumper-to-bumper on a Friday night like this.

Boze waited until they pulled up in front of the pool hall before he told Gunner. He just wanted to see his face. See how pale he would turn. See how sick and scared he would look. While they had bad reputations for being dangerous, Boze was the only truly dangerous one of the duo. And both of them knew that.

"Guess what I brought tonight?"

"What?" Gunner said.

"Guess."

"You steal some more booze from your Mom?"

"Huh-uh. Somethin' else."

"Shit, I hate guessin' games, Boze."

"My .38."

Boze got the reaction he wanted. Instant terror on Gunner's face.

"Are you crazy, man? A gun?" Gunner said.

"Scare him a little."

"You know what the cops'd do to us if they found a gun on you?"

"They've all got guns down there. We'll need one, too."

"This is the kinda shit they put you in jail for, man."

Boze was suddenly tired of Gunner's whining. Boze really was the only dangerous one here. He felt especially dangerous tonight, the .38 stuffed down the front of his jeans this way. That bastard was never going to bother Angie again, that was for sure.

"C'mon," Boze said, "let's go shoot some pool."

Boze loved the atmosphere of the place. It was mostly bikers and they looked fierce as hell in their beards and tattoos and their chains and leather vests. They never bothered Boze and Gunner either, which Boze thought was pretty cool. Just let them play. There was a good jukebox, too, a lot of heavy metal from the seventies and eighties, the only kind of rock and roll Boze could stand. No blacks.

They shot for two hours. Gunner was lame as usual. Especially so tonight. Boze could see the gun thing was really working on him. Gunner could barely concentrate on his game. Gunner kept running back to the john all the time. Pissing. Nerves.

When they were out in the night air again, leaning on the Firebird and smoking cigarettes and watching the Friday night traffic, all the beautiful wan city girls cruising past and gracing Boze and Gunner with the most disinterested of glances, and the whole city redolent of fuming ripe Indian summer, Gunner said, "Man, that gun of yours scares me."

"Don't be such a chickenshit."

"I didn't sign on for no gun, man."

"We're gonna scare him a little is all."

Gunner looked at Boze. "Really?"

"Really."

"You give me your word, Boze?"

"I give you my word."

"You better not use that thing," Gunner said. "You better not man."

Another planet.

At least that's what it felt like to Boze. Everything looked darker, for one thing. The lights in the houses didn't seem to burn quite so bright. The glow of TV sets seemed dulled, somehow. Even the headlights of the battered cars that prowled the streets like wounded animals . . . even they had a gauzy, faint cast to them. Boze had expected a lot of noise. Shadowland. Blacks dancing in the street maybe to rap music and throwing their doped-up bodies this way and that. But the streets were mostly empty. And dark. And silent. The only sound was the occasional car radio thundering rap music. Or the sound of the muffler long perforated scraping sparks on the black street.

The little houses seemed to cower in the night as they had cowered ever since they'd been built.

Another planet.

The houses small, hunched together. Large empty lots

here and there. The occasional brand new car parked proudly in a driveway. Eyes, gang eyes, peering at Boze and Gunner as they passed by in their white-boy tourist arrogance. Don't belong here motherfucker. Don't belong here. Even Boze now feeling a tightening in his groin, a hammering in his heart.

The way Boze'd known how to find the black guy was because he'd followed him. Saw the guy pulling away from the trailer one day and whipped around and followed him all the way back to Cedar Rapids. Twenty or so the guy was, no flashy black clothes bullshit or any of that. Kinda straight-looking, actually. But still a coon. Boze'd followed him right to his door. Boze wondered if he lived with his folks. Guy pulled into his driveway and never seemed to notice Boze at all. Boze just went right on by. But he sure knew where to come next time. He sure did.

This was next time.

Boze parked half a block away. They had to be careful of the gang members they'd seen here and there. Or maybe they weren't really gang members. Just kids. But kids who'd gladly whump on two country boys like themselves.

Boze figured it'd be safer if they took the alley. In the moonlight the garages spoke of other eras, dating all the way back to the twenties when cars had been big and boxy. Cats sat on garbage cans watching them. Boze whispered to them. He liked cats.

"So when we get there—" Gunner was saying.

"Real simple, man," Boze said. "When we get there, we try the back door. If his car's there, we go inside and scare the shit out of him."

"Scare him and that's all?"

"That's all."

"And if he's not there—"

"Then we leave him a note and tell him to leave Angie alone."

"I just wish you didn't have that gun, man."

"The gun's just for show, Gunner. Just fucking relax, will you?"

Boze recognized the house from the back. How many dark green houses were there on this block?

He also recognized something else. The dude's car. The same one Boze had followed here.

"The lights're out," Gunner said, as if Boze was blind and couldn't see for himself.

"Yeah," Boze said.

The lights out and Angie inside . . . Well, just as Boze wasn't blind, he also wasn't stupid. He didn't have to wonder much about what his sister was doing.

"You really sure you want to do this?" Gunner said.

"Really sure."

"I'm scared, Boze."

"You bastard."

"I can't help it. The gun and everything, man. What if he has a gun."

"Yeah, but we're gonna surprise him. He won't have time to pull a gun."

"I can't help it, Boze, I'm just scared." Gunner sounded on the edge of crying. Little-boy crying. The bogeyman was after him.

Then Gunner said, "I'm goin' back to the car, Boze."

"You're shittin' me."

"I can't do it, Boze. Not breakin' in like this. And havin' a gun and everything."

"You really are a chickenshit."

"I don't even care if I have to walk home, Boze. I'm goin'. I really am. I just don't want to do this."

Boze just shook his head, couldn't friggin' believe it, and watched Gunner walk away.

Then he sighed. He was the dangerous one, after all, and he should've realized that a long time ago. Gunner wasn't dangerous. He just liked pretending he was. But somehow Boze couldn't hate him. They'd grown up together. He said, "Just wait in the car, man. I won't be long." Gunner, shambling moon-mined against the ancient sagging garages that smelled of so many dusty and decaying decades, stopped and turned back. "You better leave this one alone, Boze, I just got a feeling. A real bad feeling. The gun and all, man. That gun's gonna get you in trouble. It really is."

Then he was gone, caught up in shadows, and then he was vanished, one with the night.

Boze took the gun from inside his belt. He was gonna scare the guy. And kick Angie's ass out. That was all. Nothing more.

He walked to the back door, ducking under a clothesline. The support poles were rusty. There were dried dog turds on the autumn-brown grass.

He heard it, then. Coming from inside. Music. Faint. Not rap but black. Definitely black. That heavy bass. That rhythm and blues beat. A sexy black song. For lovers. The fucker. The black fucker. He gripped his gun tighter.

There was a small screened-in porch, the screening old and brown and curling up from the edges. He went up on the steps and went inside. The porch was empty except for three flats of empty Budweiser cans waiting to be cashed in at a supermarket.

The music was louder. And for the first time, he heard voices. The voices were even fainter than the music. Coming from inside.

He peered between the curtains hanging in the back door.

A kitchen. Dishes piled high. Beer cans all over the place. No, the guy didn't live here with his mother. He lived here alone. Bachelor pad.

Boze tried the doorknob. Locked.

He stood still for a moment, considering the various ways he could get inside. Easiest would be just breaking down the frigging door. But he wanted to surprise the guy. Just to see his face. How scared he'd be.

Boze took out his switchblade and went to work. The lock mechanism was very old and vulnerable. There was no skill or grace in what Boze did. He simply jiggled and jammed and twisted and jabbed the point of his switchblade around inside until the doorknob turned all the way to the right. He went inside.

Cigarette smoke. Stale beer. Even staler wine. Pizza. Vomit. For sure, the guy lived alone. Nobody's mother would put up with this kind of crap.

He heard them much more clearly now. The voices. Coming from the other part of the house. Boy and girl voices. Having-sex voices. Boze felt sick.

He gripped the gun even tighter and started walking carefully through the small house. Didn't want to bang into something and give himself away. Not that they'd be able to hear. Not with the soft, sexy music going. Not with the sex they were having, the unmistakable sounds of pleasure that seemed at least occasionally to also include pain.

And then he couldn't take it anymore, couldn't take the idea of those black hands all over his little sister's white body. He jerked his gun up and ran straight into the lone bedroom off the living room. Ran straight in swearing and screaming and threatening. Ran straight in and put the gun right in the guy's face.

Right in the fucker's face.

Then all three of them were swearing and screaming.

Angie got home right at eleven o'clock, the way Mom had told her to. She was sort of drunk. Her clothes were wrinkled and her make-up was a mess.

But Boze didn't care. He just sat in the recliner staring at the TV—country western videos—and sipping from the fifth of Old Grandad he'd found up in the cupboard.

Even drunk, Angie could tell something was wrong. "You all right?"

"Yeah." But he wasn't all right and that was clear.

"I think I had too much to drink tonight."

He raised his eyes to her. "Yeah? No shit? I could hardly tell."

"I hate it when you're sarcastic."

He started watching videos again.

She stood and stared at him for a time and then she all of a sudden clamped her hand over her mouth and rushed into the bathroom and puked all over the place.

He wasn't going to help her but then he stood up anyway and went into the bathroom and took down a wash cloth and got it hot and soapy and then he wiped off her face and got her all cleaned up. She was sagging, drunk and drained, against the far wall. He got her arm around him and half-carried her into her bed. He got her dress off and put her to bed with her slip and panties. He wanted her to be a little girl again. And him to be a little boy again. But time didn't let you go back. It always pushed you on ahead in the darkness. And there was always something terrible waiting there for you in that darkness. Sometimes there were good things but they were never good enough to compensate for the bad things. For how people changed on you. For how people let you down.

He went into the bathroom and cleaned it all up.

Then he went back to the living room and sat in the recliner again and drank whiskey and stared at the TV. He should be tearing this fucking place apart is what he should be doing. But somehow he didn't have the energy.

She didn't get home until nearly three A.M.

Boze still sat in the recliner. He'd finished the bourbon and was now drinking the remnants of the scotch.

When she saw him from the doorway, she said, quietly, "I'm sorry you had to find out that way. I mean, I probably should be mad at you for breaking in that way but—"

She shook her head. She looked very sad. "Roger's a very nice guy. He comes into the restaurant all the time on his way back from Iowa City. That's how we met."

Boze looked up and smirked. "That's his name? A black guy named Roger?"

"Oh, God, Boze. He's a very nice man. He's assistant professor at Iowa."

"And he lives in a place like that, all those beer cans and stuff?"

She came into the trailer, closing the door behind her.

"He had a birthday party for his nephew earlier. That's why the mess. He'll clean it up tomorrow. He really will."

She came over to him and stood above him. "I want you to give me the gun, Boze. You terrified us tonight. I just couldn't believe it when I saw you standing there."

He looked straight up at her, all his hatred and hurt in his eyes, and said, "My own mother, sleeping with a black guy."

She slapped him, then, harder than she'd ever slapped him in her life.

Boze should have been the one who cried, the slap and all being hard.

76

But it was Mom who cried. Mom who went into the bedroom and quietly closed the door and cried and cried and cried.

Boze just sat in the living room all by himself and didn't cry at all.

A New Man

The way things worked out, it was kind of funny.

It was a warm spring day as I wheeled into town in my Ford roadster. Every once in a while I'd glance in the rear view mirror and startle myself. That doc on the West Coast had done a real good job. He'd charged too much but I didn't have much choice. I could've killed him, I suppose, but believe it or not killing doesn't come easy to me. The papers and the radio would have you believe that I kill people all the time. But that's just hooey to sell newspapers and hair tonic.

The place was the sort of dusty little town I'd expected to find along the Mississippi River on the Iowa side of the river. Three blocks of shopping, a town square with a bandstand, three or four churches, and a lot of small boats along the river, bobbing on the gentle waves. A lot of colored people along the dam, fishing. A bunch of white boys playing base-ball in the parking lot of a small factory.

And some very pretty ladies sitting at a small outdoor café drinking lemonade and smoking cigarettes and listening to Al Jolson on the radio.

Now that's the part of my reputation I don't mind. The newspapers always gussied me up as a ladies' man and I guess that's true. They say I'm good looking and while I'm not likely to argue with that, looks don't have nothing to do with my success with women. The gals like me for a simple reason:

they know I really like and respect women and know how to treat them right.

I decided to have myself a lemonade.

I carried my glass out to the porch that overlooked the river. The four gals were all in summer linen dresses the pastel colors of flowers. They all wore their hair bobbed and they all smoked like Bette Davis, you know, with her wrist angled backwards when she was just resting her cigarette. I had to smile. I was the same way. I go into a pitcher show and darned if I don't come out imitating the mannerisms of the hero. Sometimes I didn't even *know* I was doing it.

The gals looked me over and whispered and giggled among themselves like schoolgirls. They were small-town sweet and I liked them. The way they smiled at me, I guess I must've passed muster.

I sat there and enjoyed the river. Though we were in the shiny new 1930s, you could still easily imagine the old paddle wheelers making their way up here from New Orleans. Gambling boats filled with beautiful ladies and fast-shuffling men. Nights of music and reckless love. I guess every generation looks back on the previous times as better somehow.

It wasn't long before the law showed up. My instinct was to go for my gun. There were two things wrong with that. These days, I didn't carry a gun. And there wasn't any reason to get excited anyway. My new face didn't in any way resemble my old face.

He was young and he had just about the right amount of swagger. Too much and he would've been a punk and too little and he would've been a coward. He wore a khaki uniform with a bright silver badge that glared in the sun. His gun was a Colt. 45, the kind that Bob Steele and Hopalong Cassidy pack in the picture shows. He was probably 25 and except for a broken nose he looked like a magazine cover. The altar boy ten years later.

He sat down. Didn't ask. Just sat down. He wore a white Stetson and doffed it to the gals. He must've passed muster, too. They sent him several flirtatious smiles, little invisible valentines.

"Those're the kind of gals who could get a married man in trouble," he said.

He was drinking lemonade, too.

"I imagine that's true."

He pushed his hand across the table to me. He had a strong but easy hand. He wasn't trying to impress anybody. "Name's Swenson. Con Swenson. I'm the acting sheriff. Hasty, Bob Hasty the sheriff, he's laid up with some kinda heart condition so I been sort of running things for the past two months. And you'd be?"

"Paul Caine."

"And Paul Caine would be from?"

"Milwaukee. I sell kitchen appliances there."

He nodded. "I've got a wife who's got every one of 'em. You should see our place." Then—still and always a lawman —"You're just passing through?"

"Staying a few days then going on to Cedar Rapids. Got a cousin there. But he won't be back for a couple of days so I thought I'd stay here and fish. Hear it's good here."

"Real good. Best fishing in the state except up near Devil's Backbone and a few places like that." Then: "Know anybody here?"

"Not a soul."

He watched my face, my hands, the way I moved. I knew I'd passed muster with the gals. With him I wasn't sure.

"You find a hotel yet?"

"Not yet."

"Hell, then, let me take you over to the Paladium. My

cousin Ned is the desk clerk there. I'll get you a deal on a room. And it'll be a nice one, too."

I smiled. "You're a little bit of Chamber of Commerce, too?"

"Not Chamber. Not yet. But Jaycee and Rotary. Sheriff thinks we need to be part of our community and I agree with him. The days of a peace officer just totin' a gun around and tryin' to scare people are over. At least around these parts. C'mon, I'll walk over with you."

He was a strange one for a copper and he made me uneasy. I don't think he'd figured out who I was or what I was doing here. But something else was going on and I wondered what it was.

I grabbed my one suitcase from the car and we walked a block east. There sure were a lot of pretty girls here. Wagons went by, horses hot in the Iowa sun, leaving sweet-scented fly-specked remnants of their passage in the road. Roadsters went by; trucks went by; a big Packard with some fancy people in the back and Chicago plates went by. "Flying Down To Rio" with Ginger Rogers and Fred Astaire was on the picture show marquee.

The Paladium was on the other side of the street and just as we were approaching it, a woman was coming out of a dress shop next door. I couldn't get a good look at her.

When Swenson saw her, he shouted, "Hey, honey!"

And then she turned toward us and squinted into the sun. And then her pretty face ignited into a smile and she returned the wave. And then went on walking in the opposite direction.

"That's the little woman," Swenson said. "My wife."

"Pretty," I said.

"She sure is," he said proudly. "I hope you get a chance to meet her."

But I had met her. Many times I'd met her. And that was why, in fact, I was here. Because I'd met her and she'd betrayed me and now I was going to kill her.

The fishing turned out to be all I'd heard. I spent two days collecting sunrays and catfish, and two nights drinking bathtub gin and squiring about a young woman who wore just a wee bit too many pieces of Kleenex in her bra. But her earnestness endeared her to me, and so we spent several sweet moonlit hours in a hushed cove next to where the water ran moonsilver at midnight.

Not until Tuesday did I start following the lawman's wife. When I'd known her her name had been Ann Sage and she'd lived in Chicago. Here her name was Karen Caine. She'd put on ten pounds and dipped her hair a little too often in the peroxide bottle. She had a nice life. During the day, she went to the beauty shop and the picture show and the bakery.

Nights, her appointed rounds became even more interesting. I found a hill on the right side of the isolated Caine house on the edge of town. Through my field glasses, I saw that hubby, apparently tired, usually went to bed around 8:30, leaving Karen downstairs to read movie magazines, smoke Chesterfields and listen to the radio.

He came from the woods in back of the house, her lover. He was a big man with a handsome but fierce face and a lot of girly-curly dark hair. He went straight into the darkened garage. She came out promptly at ten. It was all pretty sensible, when you thought about it. You go anywhere with somebody, folks are bound to see you eventually. But if all you do is go out to your garage—and she carried a small sack of garbage as a pretext—who could see anything? If lover boy kept his mouth shut, who would ever know?

And hubby was upstairs asleep.

★ ★ ★ ★ ★

On my fourth day in town, I rolled out of bed an hour later than usual. That bathtub gin can do bad things to your system, especially your head.

He knocked and then came right in without my invitation. He had on a crisp new khaki uniform that would be sweated out and dusted out by day's end and he had this strange smile on his face. One of those smug smiles that said he knew something I didn't.

"Morning," he said.

"Morning," I said, still in my boxers, still sitting on the side of my single bed. I fired up a Lucky.

He had a glass in his hand. A plain 6-ounce drinking glass.

"Recognize this?" he said.

Something was sure up. He was so excited he kept licking his lips and breathing very hard.

"Looks like a glass to me."

"Yeah, but what kinda glass?"

"Drinking glass." The hangover had left me irritable. "Look, I always like to have some breakfast before I play parlor games."

The grin came—full force now. "This ain't no parlor game I'm playing, Mr. Dillinger."

So then I knew. "The glass I drank lemonade from?"

"One and the same."

"You're a bright lad."

"Bright enough to match the fingerprints with the WANTED poster J. Edgar sent out when they thought you were still alive. I didn't know who you were so I had to look through a lot of posters. You got a real funny whorl on your right thumb."

"I cut it on a scythe when I was a kid."

"Too bad. It's real easy to spot you."

"You tell them where they can find me?"

His wife Anne Sage had told the federales where they could find me on the night of July 22. She'd be wearing red when we left the theater and she'd be standing next to me. She'd pitch to the left and they'd open fire. What they hadn't counted on was me figuring that something was going on. She'd been acting jittery all night. Just as we were leaving the theater, I grabbed her and used her as a shield. J. Edgar wouldn't want his boys to gun down an innocent girl. It'd look bad in the press. So they didn't have any choice but to let me get in my car—her along for the ride—and get away. That was three years ago. Since then that West Coast doc had worked on my face, turning me into a new man. And I'd been looking for Ann Sage.

Or had been.

I'd outrun J. Edgar once. I doubted I'd do it again.

"They've probably got this hotel surrounded," I said, suddenly feeling a lot wearier than my thirty-seven years.

He shook his head. "Nah. I haven't called them yet."

I took a deep drag of the Lucky. The stream of smoke I exhaled was a perfect ice blue. Beautiful in its way. "You want all the glory for yourself, huh? 'I Captured John Dillinger.' Make you a regular folk hero."

He looked kind of dopey then. And I realized just how young and unsophisticated he was. Despite all the tough talk, I mean.

Standing right there, a badge on his chest, a gun on his hip, for all the world a cold and serious lawman, he got tears in his eyes and said, "I can't take it anymore, Mr. Dillinger."

"Can't take what?" I said.

So he told me.

I slept in again the next morning. This time it wasn't the

fault of bathtub gin. I was just tired. It'd been a long and industrious night.

The desk clerk, as I handed him the two dollars I owed him for my last night, said, "You must've slept through all the excitement."

"Oh?"

"You met Deputy Caine."

"Sure. Nice young man."

The clerk, who had a mole, slick hair and breath that could peel onions, leaned forward on the desk and said, "His old lady was bangin' this here young buck of a farmer, see? The way folks surmise it is the farmer wanted her to leave Caine and marry him. They musta had an argument, see, and the farmer killed her and then hisself."

I shook my head. "Boy, what a sad old world."

"I hear ya, brother." Then: "Caine didn't hear about it till this morning. He took a prisoner over to Dunkertown and stayed there all night right on a cot in the police station."

Hard to find a better alibi than that.

I was just tossing my bag in my roadster when I saw Deputy Caine coming out of his office and walking into the dusty street. Several people stopped him. The way they kind of whispered and gently touched him, you could tell they were trying to console him.

I whipped the roadster around so that I'd drive past the sheriff's office as I left town. When I got even with the small stone building, I stepped on the brake. Caine came over and put his foot on the running board.

"I guess we both got what we wanted," he said.

I guess we did. She'd betrayed me with the feds and she'd betrayed him in bed. We'd both gotten what we wanted.

"So everything go all right?"

"Just fine." The farmer had been big, all right, but dumb.

Faking his suicide hadn't been difficult at all.

"She say anything, you know, before she died?"

I knew what he wanted to hear. What any man would want to hear. That she was sorry she betrayed him. That she still loved him.

"I could lie to you, kid, but I'm not sure I'd be doing you any favors."

"Yeah, I suppose not." He squinted up at the sun. "That funeral parlor's gonna be hot as a bitch tonight, with the wake and all."

"Yeah," I said.

Hot as a bitch.

"Good luck with everything—Mr. Thompson," he said. And grinned.

That had been my part of the bargain. I kill his wife for him —something he couldn't bring himself to do—and he let me go without informing the feds. Seemed reasonable to me.

"Good luck to you, too, Deputy."

We shook hands. Then I gave the roadster some gas. With any luck I'd be in central Iowa by nightfall.

Judgment

The man had been standing here for twenty minutes, just after dusk, just after the rain began. The drops were silver in the dirty light of the street lamp. It was chill enough, this late April, to tint the man's cheeks a winter red and make his nose run.

Dressed as he was in a dark cap and dark topcoat and dark slacks, the man was nearly invisible in the gloom. Not that he had to worry much about being seen. This part of the city was being torn down, hundred-year-old houses leveled and many of the rest boarded up. Only a few people lived here anymore, and most of them were the homeless who huddled in the corners of empty houses shivering against the cold in their rags and gloves with missing fingers, drinking cheap wine that was as bitter as lighter fluid.

The house the man stared at was boarded up, but on the second floor you could see a faint light between the boards over the windows. At one time the place had been a respectable two-story white frame house. Husbands and wives and kids and dreams had lived here, but no longer. Now just a man named McLennan walked its floors.

A car went by, the sort of car you'd expect to see in this neighborhood, a big old dinosaur a dozen years old with a smashed windshield and cancerous rust everywhere and a rumbling muffler in bad need of replacement and three teenagers in the front seat giggling behind pot and beer.

Nicholas Ryan stepped out of the light till the car got past and then he walked quickly through the dirty puddles in the middle of the street.

Rain spraying his face, Ryan hurried onto the lawn of the house and then moved in the shadows along the side of the place. Two or three times he felt his foot slide into dog shit and once he crushed the ragged neck of a broken beer bottle. The once-white siding was now covered with rust stains, as if it were bleeding.

Ryan took the stairs leading up the side of the house. Whipping wind covered any noise he made.

When he reached the top step, he put his head close to the torn screen door and listened. He heard nothing. McLennan was an alcoholic who started drinking right after he got off his factory job. He was usually passed out by now. That's what Ryan was counting on, anyway.

The door was easy to push open, the inside lock hanging at an angle just as Ryan remembered.

A minute later, he stood inside.

During the last of its years, the house had been rented out as two large apartments, upstairs and downstairs. Ryan just hoped the downstairs looked better than this.

The upstairs consisted of a single large room plus a bathroom and a tiny room for storage. The furniture had all come from Goodwill, sprung purple couch and wobbly blond coffee table and any number of knickknacks that were embarrassing to behold, not least the hula-girl lamp on one of the end tables. The faded floral wallpaper was peeling, and ran with the same sort of stain as the white siding.

The floor was an obstacle course of empty beer cans, pizza cardboards, dirty socks, dirty underwear, gigantic dust balls, steel-toed work shoes, and endless empty gnarled-up cigarette packages.

If only I could count on him getting lung cancer, Ryan noted ruefully.

But the smell was worst of all. It was the smell of mildew and age and dust and dirt and shit and piss and sweat; and the smell of perversion. Ryan could think of no other way to characterize it. This large squalid room reeked of a decadence that almost made him vomit. He wanted to get out of here as soon as he could.

Richard McLennan had the ancient Motorola TV console and the purple couch and the overstuffed armchair with the filthy orange slipcovers and the blond coffee table arranged so that it all fit together like a tiny living room. He could sit in the chair with his feet on the coffee table guzzling beer after beer and watching the black and white 21" Motorola TV screen.

Next to the chair was a cardboard box, and Ryan knew right away that this was what he was looking for. The proof he needed.

Before seating himself and going through the box, he walked over to the far east corner of the room where the single bed was pushed up against the wall and where McLennan lay snoring. Above the bed was a cheap plastic crucifix, Christ dying endlessly. A crucifix did not belong in such a room. Ryan wanted to tear it from the wall.

Ryan stood above the bed and looked down at the man. He was really pretty nondescript, McLennan. Fleshy but not fat; unpleasant-looking (always needed a shave and a haircut) but not ugly; middle-aged but not really aged. Now, lying among sheets that hadn't been washed or straightened out in a long time, McLennan slept with a brown quart bottle of beer clutched in his right hand. The beer had spilled on the bed. McLennan lay face-up, his snoring a wet ugly sound.

Ryan, assuming McLennan wasn't going to wake up, went

back to the chair. He sat on the edge of it and picked up the cardboard box.

The first picture was a Polaroid color shot. It showed a girl approximately six years old standing completely naked and staring at the camera. She had some kind of dog collar around her neck. In the right of the photo you could see a whip dangling. It looked like a long black terrible snake. The little girl's expression was blank. She had probably been drugged.

The next photograph he found was of a little boy and a dog and—

Sickened, Ryan tossed the photo back into the box and set the box back down. There would be hundreds of such photographs in the box, every sort of little boy and girl, every imaginable configuration and position and perversion and—

Ryan put his face in his hands and began drawing deep, deep breaths. He wanted to smell clean, fresh air. It would be good to stand outside again in the chill night. Be reinvigorated. Redeemed. This place and all it represented was beginning to overpower him. Over there in the west corner was where the photo of the little girl and the whips had been taken. He tried not to think of what had become of her after McLennan was done with her. What had happened to any of the children.

He went straight over to the bed now and took out the Walther and fitted the silencer to it and then put the weapon right against the center of McLennan's forehead.

Ryan said, "Wake up."

After a time, the snoring spluttered to a stop and McLennan's sad frantic brown eyes showed themselves.

He was still drunk—his rank breath overwhelming even from this distance—but not so drunk that he didn't understand immediately what was going on.

"Hey!" he said. "What the hell's happening here?"

He tried to jump up from bed. Ryan kept the muzzle of the Walther tight against his forehead.

"You didn't stop the way you promised, did you?" Ryan said.

"Hey, what the hell're you doing here? You think I don't know who you are and what you are?"

"You promised me, McLennan. You promised me you'd stop or get help."

"You can't do this. You're a—"

But before he could get the word out, Ryan killed him. A single bullet straight into the brain.

A small gelatinous embryo was borne out the back of McLennan's head. He jerked and jumped as if he'd been electrocuted and then he lay quite still. The air smelled of the gunshot and blood and of McLennan shitting his pants.

Ryan raised his hand and made the sign of the cross and then said some words in Latin. He still preferred Latin.

Before he left he dumped the cardboard box in the sink and took lighter fluid and burned all the photographs.

"Bless me Father for I have sinned. It's been three weeks since my last confession."

"Go on. Confess your sins."

"I killed a man tonight, Father."

There was a long silence in the darkness of the confessional. In the shadows on the other side of the curtain the old priest sighed. On the air was the sweet scent of incense. It was nearly nine o'clock on a Saturday night. The church empty except for a lone old lady who knelt beneath her bright ethnic headscarf far ahead at the communion rail.

The old priest sighed again. "It's you, isn't it, Father Ryan?"

"Yes, Father, it is."

"This is the third time you've confessed to me in a year."

"Yes, Father."

"Yet you continue to kill people."

"Only those who won't help themselves or seek help from others. The man I killed tonight confessed to me once a month that he had molested children. I told him to stop, I told him where he could find psychiatric help. But he did nothing to help himself." He paused. "We've taken the vow of silence, Father. I couldn't turn him in. I stopped him the only way I could—before he hurt any other children."

"And the two others you killed?"

"An arsonist who set several fires that killed people, and a rapist who mutilated his victims afterward."

"And you could find no other way to stop them, Father Ryan?"

"No other way. Otherwise they would continue to kill people."

In the vast shadows of the church, the old woman at the communion rail coughed. The sound reminded Ryan of a gunshot.

"Are you sorry for your sins, Father Ryan?"

"I want to be sorry, Father."

"Then pray with me that you never again do such a thing."

"Yes, Father."

"Pray with me now, Father Ryan. Pray harder than you ever have in your life, Father Ryan."

"Yes, Father. I will. I promise. Harder than I ever have in my life."

Three weeks later, the man came back to Father Ryan. Late on a Saturday night. Father Ryan in his confessional. Only a few people left kneeling before the flickering green and yellow and blue votive candles.

Father Ryan recognized the voice immediately.

"Forgive me, Father, for I have sinned."

"Go on. Tell me your sins."

A pause. "My daughter, Father. She's ten and I—"

"Yes?"

"I force her to have sex with me."

"I see." Trying to control his anger, Father Ryan said, "You've been here before."

"Yes, Father."

"Confessing the same sin."

"Yes, Father."

"And I've told you about the psychology clinic over on Third Avenue by the railroad tracks."

"Yes, Father."

"How it's free and confidential."

"Yes, Father."

"Have you gone there yet?"

"No, Father."

"But in the meantime, you've molested your daughter again?"

"Yes, Father."

Father Ryan said nothing. "Are you going to go to the clinic?"

"Yes, Father."

"You absolutely promise me?"

"Yes, Father."

Father Ryan heard the rest of the man's sins and then gave him his penance.

When he left, the man sounded quite sorry about what he'd done.

Father Ryan had to hurry. Slip out the side door to the

parking lot and catch a glimpse of the man and the car he was driving.

Father Ryan stood in the shadows of the church door watching a nice-looking man in a three-piece-suit get into a small sports car. Father Ryan, who had a good memory for figures, noted the man's license number.

Sadly, turning back to the interior of his church, Father Ryan knew that he would soon enough be using the man's license number as he set about investigating the man just as he'd first investigated McLennan and the two others.

Father Ryan, alone in the church now, went to the communion rail and prayed long into the night.

Ghosts

Some nights were kinder to thieves than others.

Tonight, for instance. The October Saturday was prisoner to chill rain and rolling fog. All kinds of things could hide in such darkness.

The convenience store was an oasis in the gloom, windows bright with neon letters blue and green and red advertising various beers and wine, parking lot filled with the battered cars of the working poor, cracked windshields and primer-gray spots covering up damaged fenders and doors and leaking exhaust systems that shook the vehicles in orgasmic spasms, black radios booming rap, white radios booming heavy metal.

Byrnes was of the night and the fog itself, the damp slimy fog encircling him like glistening nightmare snakes, his own dark eyes glistening, too, anger, fear, need, loneliness, and a strange dreamy feeling, as if he were detached from himself, just watching this dumb pathetic fuck named Byrnes do all this stuff:

The night smelled of coldness and traffic fumes and his own harsh cigarette breath. He was trembling.

He stood across the street from the store, black coat, black gloves, black jeans, black high-top running shoes, just the way he'd learned in prison up to Anamosa. Five-to-ten armed robbery. But because of his young age—and because of overcrowding—he'd served only four.

He'd been out six months. His young wife was gone, the baby she used to bring to the prison and claim was his, the baby gone, too. First month or so he'd been a Boy Scout. Did everything his parole officer told him. Showed up nice and regular at the job at a wholesale tire company where he put outsize rubber on truck fleets and big-ass farm equipment. Got himself a respectable little sleeping room. Stayed away from his old crowd. Even went to mass a few times.

Then Heather, this chick he met down to this Black Crows concert at the Five Seasons, she turned him on to meth and man, he hadn't been straight a moment since. Now, he was lucky if he dragged himself into work two, three days a week. Once a month, his parole officer checked with his employer, see how Byrnes was doing. Pretty soon it would be his ass. The parole officer would demand a urine test and they'd find the meth in Byrnes and he'd be back in the joint for parole violation.

His only hope was to get enough money to lay by a few weeks' supply of meth and then head for the yards down by Quaker Oats. In the joint there'd been a lot of talk about bein' a hobo. The stories you heard in prison you had to cut in half —nobody loved to bullshit you as much as bored cons—but even cut in half the life of a 'bo sounded pretty cool. The idea of waking up in a gondola on a beautiful warm morning out in the west somewhere . . . and the life would be so healthy, he'd even be able to kick meth too. He'd be free again in all senses.

He had to stand there nearly forty-five minutes before the lull came. He'd hit eight stores in the past seven weeks and by now, he knew their patterns pretty good. Even the busiest convenience store had a lull. Even on a Saturday night. This store was having a lull now, parking lot empty, clerk working on a counter display.

Byrnes gripped the .45 in the pocket of his cheap black

raincoat and walked across the rain-glistening street.

Clerk was a black woman in the orange polyester uniform jacket and silly hat Happy Campers made all their employees wear, the orange only emphasizing her already considerable size. She looked smart and friendly, smiling silently at him as he walked to the coolers in the back where the beer was kept. He was quickly checking to see if any customers were lurking unseen back there. None were.

He went right up front and pulled the gun and said, "Just make this easy for us, all right?"

She did something he wouldn't have expected. She smiled. Couple gold teeth, she had, and she smiled with them. She smelled good, a heady, spicy perfume. "You look more scared than I do."

"I just want the money, ma'am. Just please make it easy for both of us. All right?"

She glanced at the cash register. "Most I got in there is five, six hundred."

"Give me everything you've got in there. Now."

She sighed. "You're shakin', boy. You know that?" There was real pity in her eyes and voice. "I got a boy about your age. I sure hope he never do nothin' like you're doin'."

The car was in the parking lot, then, the beam of its headlights playing across the wall behind the clerk.

She'd been talking too much. Lulls never lasted long. She'd been talking too much and he hadn't stopped her. And now there was a car pulling in the lot.

"You better get your ass out of here," she said. "And hurry."

He couldn't believe it. She didn't seem intimidated at all by the gun. Or his black getup.

He said, "I just got out of prison, lady."

She grinned. "I did time myself. Now you git, you hear me?"

Thunk of a heavy car door slamming. Then a second door shutting. Two people at least. Coming inside. Quickly.

"And lemme do you a favor and take that before you hurt somebody."

His mind was divided, part of it on the door and the two figures now outlined inside the fog. The other part watching as the woman reached out—slo-mo, just like in the movies—and started to take the .45 from him.

"Hey!" he said, wanting to cry out in frustration and bafflement.

The door opening. Two balding, middle-aged men coming in. And the clerk grasping the gun and twisting it to get it away from him.

And him so startled and angry and—

He fired twice.

He would never know if he'd actually meant to fire. Or if it had just been a terrible accident. He could never be sure.

He'd never seen anybody shot before. TV had conditioned him to expect an imposing and dramatic moment. But all she did, really, was put big hard-working black hands over the blood patches in the front of her silly Happy Camper orange uniform jacket.

There was this terrible silence—it couldn't have lasted more than a second or two—and inside it he could hear her start to sob. She was dying. He had no doubt about that and neither did she.

And then there was no room for silence in the store as the men crashed into aisles trying to find a safe place from his weapon. And him firing to keep them at bay. And then her screaming as she started to fall over backwards into the silver ice cream machine.

And then he was running, too. He didn't know where. Just running and running and running and the fog made it a bitch running you can believe that running into a tree once and stumbling over a sidewalk crack another time and then tripping over a tiny tricycle another time palms all cut to shit from the sidewalk and all the time cursing and sobbing and seeing her die there over and over and over seeing her die had he really shot her on purpose? Her dying over and over and over.

And him running through this Midwestern night and sirens now and fog heavier now a half-world really not the real world at all half-world and faint half-lighted windows and half-voices in the houses and apartments lost in the gloom muted cries of infants and lusting lovers and angry lovers and droning TVs and him nothing more than slapping footsteps and whining searing breath in the windpipe in the night. Alone . . .

He made no conscious effort to reach this place. And when he saw it he had to smile. Maybe he wasn't as luckless as he'd thought.

Not easy to see the railroad yard in the fog. But he could make out the general shape of it. Smell the oil and heat and damp steel of it. See the vast brick roundhouse and the two-story barracks-like building where business was conducted during the day. The crosshatching of silver track. And the box cars, walls of them lined up into infinity into the fog and the night, unseen engines down the line, rumbling and shuddering and thrumming in this half-world like great beasts of a prehistoric time, unseen but all-powerful as they stole a line of boxcars here and a line of boxcars there, and began moving them into the Midwestern night borne for places as forlorn as Utah and as magnificent as California, and hoboes of every description (if prison talk was to be believed) riding fine and happy inside the dark empty wombs of them.

Riding fine and happy.

He'd be doing that himself in a few minutes.

Three hours ago, Chicago Mike had enjoyed a gourmet meal at the local Salvation Army. Chicken and peas and mashed potatoes. This was a good town, far as free food went. He'd been planning on staying a few nights but the place was full up and they had to put the extras in this little building away from the main action where all of Chicago Mike's friends were so he just decided to head back to the yard from whence he came and find a westbound train. He had to ask one of the yard clerks for help. Chicago Mike, a scruffy sixty-six years of age, could remember the days when rail workers had been the enemy. No more. They hated management so much for always trying to bust their unions that they were happy to help 'bos with information. A railroad dick tonight even walked Chicago Mike to a newish car and helped him up on it. Long long ago—back in the days when he still had teeth and had an erection at least once a day— Chicago Mike had busted his knee up hopping a freight and he'd moved real slow and ginger ever since.

He was ensconced now for the night. Tucked into a corner of the big car. He'd taken an apple and a Snickers from the Salvation Army. He figured these'd make a good breakfast. He had his .38 stuffed under his right thigh. Sometimes, you'd fall asleep and find yourself with unwanted company, a 'bo with bad manners or murderous intent. There were gangs on the rails these days, and they'd kill you just for pleasure. He threw his blanket over his legs and hunched down inside his heavily layered clothes. If it got real cold, he'd get inside his sleeping bag. Two things a 'bo needed to learn real good and they were patience and how to deal with loneliness. Long time ago somebody had taught him how to summon and while most 'bos didn't believe in it, nobody knew better than Chicago Mike just how real summoning was . . .

He wasn't sure just when the kid hopped on board, Chicago Mike. He'd been in a kind of half-sleep, a sweet soft summer dream of he and his wife Kitty on the pier in Chicago 1958, just after he'd put in his Navy years. Could there ever have been a woman as pretty and gentle and loving as Kitty? Fourteen years they'd been together until that night, dancing in his arms on a dance boat, she'd slumped forward and died. Aneurysm, the docs said later. And so, after burying her, Michael Thomas Callahan, respectable purveyor of appliances to the public in Oak Park, Illinois, became Chicago Mike, rider of the rails. For years, Chicago Mike believed that only in distance and the violent metal thrashing of speeding boxcars could he find solace . . . And then he'd learned about summoning . . .

The kid huddled in the far corner of the big, empty car with the wooden floor and the metal walls defaced in spots with some singularly uncreative graffiti. Trouble, Chicago Mike knew instantly. He'd been too long atraveling not to recognize it. Trouble. He wondered what the kid had done. Robbery, at least. You didn't hop a freight for anything less. Maybe even murder.

Chicago Mike took out his long black flashlight and beamed it on the kid. "You all right, son?"

"Just leave me alone, old man."

"Most of the people on the rails, they try to be friendly and help each other."

"Good for them."

Chicago Mike clipped off his flashlight. In a few minutes, the train started to move. And then they were in the prairie night and really rolling. Chicago Mike worried vaguely about the kid jumping him—scared people were dangerous people, and this kid was definitely scared. But he wasn't worried enough to stay awake. Chicago Mike dozed off.

The scream woke him. The kid's scream.

Chicago Mike pulled himself up straight, grabbed his light and shone it on the kid.

The way the kid looked, the way he was shaking, the way his face gleamed with sweat and his eyes were wide with frantic fear . . . Chicago Mike could pretty much guess what had happened.

He stood up and walked the length of the rocking car. He moved slowly, his busted-up knee and all. The kid opened his mouth a couple times, as if he was going to tell Chicago Mike to stay away, but he ended up not saying anything at all.

Chicago Mike sat down next to the kid and handed him the pint of cheap whiskey. The kid took it and gunned himself three quick drinks.

"What kind of trouble you in, son?"

The kid just glared at him. "I didn't ask you to come over here, old man."

"No, I reckon you didn't."

"And I don't want you hangin' around."

"All right, son, if that's the way you feel."

Chicago Mike started to push himself to his feet, arthritic bones cracking. The kid grabbed his arm.

"I shouldn't be in the trouble I am," he said. "I just meant to rob the place is all."

"But somethin' else happened, huh?"

The kid looked miserable, lost. "Yeah, somethin' else happened, all right."

Chicago Mike knew not to ask any more questions. The kid would tell him what he wanted to tell him. Nothing more.

"And then I had this—nightmare, I guess you'd call it," the kid said. "Just now, when I was asleep. She—the black woman—she was in it and she was trying to get me to come with her. You know—to die."

The kid leaned his head back against the wall. Closed his eyes. The door was partly open so you could smell the cold autumn night and see the quarter moon above the cornfields. The kid said, "But that wasn't all. When I woke up—I could smell her perfume. I still can." The kid sat up and looked at Chicago Mike and said, "You know what that means? That I could smell her perfume?"

"What?"

"She was here. Right in this boxcar." He trembled. "Right in this boxcar, tryin' to get to me." He paused. "Her ghost."

"You think ghosts still have their perfume?"

"Hers did."

The pint of whiskey sat between them. Without asking, the kid picked up the pint and drained off a couple more good ones. "I appreciate it."

"My pleasure."

"You mind if I ask you to go back now?"

"No problem."

"Thanks again."

Somewhere in the night, somewhere near the Nebraska border, another scream woke Chicago Mike. But this time when he woke up, he saw the kid standing up and walking across the swaying boxcar.

"Leave me alone! Leave me alone!" the kid was shrieking.

And then he was firing the gun in his hand.

Chicago Mike had to put it together fast. Kid sees the ghost again. Grabs his gun. Starts firing. Two things wrong with that, one being that there's no way you can kill a ghost, the other being that the kid, not seeing what he's doing, is firing right at Chicago Mike.

"Kid! Kid!" Chicago Mike shouted, trying to free the kid

from his nightmare. "Quit firing your gun!"

But the bullets kept coming. Chicago Mike rolled to his right, grabbing his .38 as he did so.

The kid couldn't have many rounds left but he continued to fire right at where Chicago Mike was. The kid was screaming at the ghost all the time. Telling her to leave him alone. Telling her it was an accident. Telling her he was sorry. All the time firing.

"Kid! Kid! Quit shooting at her!"

A bullet took a piece of fabric off Chicago Mike's jacket. And then he knew he had no choice—he had to fire back, injure the kid enough to disarm him.

But just as he fired, the train rolled around a long, steep bank and Chicago Mike's shooting was thrown off: He'd meant to hit the kid in the arm. Instead, the bullet moved over and took the kid in the heart.

The kid went over backwards, kind of a Three Stooges thing actually, bouncing off the wall only to pitch forward, arms windmilling, to run head first into the other wall as the train continued to curve around the steep bank. Then he did a little pirouette in the middle of the car, and fell forward. And died.

There would be too many questions if Chicago Mike was found in a box car with a dead young man. Somewhere near Plattville, Chicago Mike pushed the kid out the door. He watched as the body hit the side of the tracks and sprawled on its back.

He'd seen it before, Chicago Mike, how a kid's first encounter with a ghost made him literally crazy. He didn't understand that the ghost didn't have any power to kill him. She was just angry that he'd killed her. Her soul hadn't passed over yet. That would happen in a day or so and then she'd forget all about him.

Chicago Mike remembered the first time he'd seen a ghost. What a wondrous experience that had been. It'd happened right after the old 'bo had taught him how to summon.

As Chicago Mike was doing right now.

He felt plain terrible about having to kill the kid. He needed a gentle and loving person to talk to.

And so he summoned. Closed his eyes as if in prayer and said the words the old 'bo had taught him.

And when he opened them again, there she was, pretty as she'd been back in 1958, the year he'd married her. His lovely wife Kitty.

She knelt next to him and kissed him and then just held him for a long time. He told her about what he'd been doing and how awful it had been accidentally killing that young kid, and then they just sat together holding hands and listening to the train spectral as the night itself, rushing into the solace of darkness.

That Day at Eagle's Point

The day was dark suddenly, even though it was only four in the afternoon, and lightning like silver spider's legs began to walk across the landscape of farm fields and county highways. It was summer, and kids would be playing near creeks and forests and old deserted barns, and their mothers would see the roiling sky and begin calling frantically for them, trying to be heard above the chill damp sudden wind.

The rains came, then, hard slanting Midwestern rains that made me feel snug inside my new Plymouth sedan, rains making noises on the hood and roof like the music of tin drums.

That was the funny thing, I told Marcie I was buying the Plymouth for her, and she even went down and picked out the model and the color all by herself, but even so, a couple of weeks later, she left. Got home one day and saw two suitcases sitting at the front door, and then came Marcie walking out of the bedroom, prettier than I'd seen her in years. "I'm going to do it, Earle," was all she said. And then there was a cab there, and he was honking, and then she was gone.

I didn't handle it so well at first. I just read and reread the letter she left, trying to divine things implied, or things written between the lines, sort of like those Dead Sea scholars spending their whole lives poring over only a few pages.

Her big hangup was Susan Finlay, and how I'd never really gotten over her, and how there was something sick about how I couldn't let go of that gal, and how she, Marcie, wanted somebody to really love her completely, the way I never could because of my lifelong "obsession" with Susan Finlay.

That was a year ago. She only called once, from a bar somewhere with a loud country-western jukebox, said she was drunk and missed me terribly but knew that for me there'd never be anybody but Susan, and she was sorry for both of us that I'd never been able to love her in the good and proper way she'd wanted.

Another thing she hadn't liked was my occupation. Over in Nam, I was with a medical unit, so when I got back to New Hope, the town where I was raised, I just naturally looked for work at the hospital. But the hospital per se wasn't hiring, so they put me in touch with the two fellows who ran the ambulance service. I became their night driver, four to midnight, six nights a week. The benefits were good, and I got to learn a lot about medicine. In the beginning, Marcie was proud of me, I think. At parties and family reunions, people always came up to me and wanted to know if I had any new ambulance stories. Old ladies seemed to have a particular fascination with the really grim ones. Marcie liked me being the one people sought out.

But then my novelty faded, and there I was just this Nam vet with the long hair and Mexican bandit mustache, and a little potbelly, and glasses as thick as Palomars, bad eyesight being a family curse. Forty-three years old, I was, time to get a real job, everybody said. But this *was* my real job, and it was likely to be my real job the rest of my life . . .

I'd hoped to catch a good glimpse of the hills on the drive up this late afternoon. The hills were where David and Susan and I liked to play. This was Carstairs, the town I grew up in and lived in till the year before they shipped me off to New

Hope. Dad got the lung disease, and Mom felt it was safer to live in New Hope where they had better hospital facilities.

But in my heart, Carstairs would always be my hometown, the town square with the bandstand and the pigeons sitting atop the Civil War monuments, and the old men playing checkers while the little kids splashed in the hot summer wading pool. If I tried hard enough, I could even smell the creosote on the railroad ties as Susan and David and I ran along the tracks looking for something to do.

The three of us grew up in the same apartment house, an old stucco thing with a gnarled and rusty TV antenna on the roof and a brown faded front lawn mined with dog turds. We were six years old the first time we ever played with each other.

We had identical lives. Our fathers were laborers, our mothers took whatever kinds of jobs they could find—dime store clerking, mostly—and we had too many brothers and too many sisters, and sometimes between the liquor and the poverty, our fathers would beat on our mothers for a time, and the "rich" kids at school—anybody who lived in an actual house was rich—the rich kids shunned us. Or shunned David and me, anyway. By the time Susan was ten, she started working her way through all the rich boys, breaking their hearts one at a time with that sad but fetching little face of hers.

But Susan had no interest in those boys, not really. Her only interest was in David and me. And David and I were interested only in Susan.

I was jealous of David. He had all the things I did not, looks, poise, mischievous charm, and curly black hair that Susan always seemed to find an excuse to touch.

I guess I started thinking about that when I was eleven or so. You always saw the older kids start pairing off about the time they reached fourteen. But who was going to pair off with Susan when we got to be fifteen—David or me? Sometimes she seemed to like David a little more than me; other times she seemed to like me a little more than David.

Then one day, when we were thirteen, I came late up to Eagle's Point, and when I got there, I saw them kissing. It looked kind of comic, actually, they didn't kiss the way movie stars did, they just kind of groped each other awkwardly. But it was enough to make me run over and tear him from her and push him back to the edge of the cliff. The fall would have killed him, and right then that was what I wanted to do, take his life. I pushed him out over the cliff, so he could get a good look at the asphalt below. All that kept him from falling was the grip I had on the sleeve of his shirt.

But then Susan was there, crying and screaming and pounding on me to pull him back before it was too late.

I'd never seen her that upset. She looked crazed. I pulled him back.

I didn't speak to either of them for a few months. I mostly stayed home and read science fiction novels. I'd discovered Ray Bradbury that spring.

School started again, and David could be seen in the halls with this cute new girl. I started hanging around Susan again. If she was sad about David, she never let on. She even asked me to go to the movies with her a couple of times. David kept hanging around the cute new girl.

In October, the jack-o'-lanterns on the porches already, I went to Susan's house one day. I kind of wanted to surprise her, have her go over town with me. Nobody answered my knock. Both the truck and the car her folks drove were gone. I tried the kitchen door. It was open. I figured I'd go in and call out her name. She slept in some Saturday mornings.

That's when I heard the noise. I guess I knew what it was, I mean it's pretty unmistakable, but I didn't want to admit it to myself.

I didn't want to sneak up the stairs, but I knew I had to. I had to know for absolutely sure.

And that's what happened. I found out. For absolutely sure.

They were making love. I tried not to think of it as "fucking" because I didn't want to think of Susan that way. I loved her too much.

"Oh, David, I love you so much," Susan said.

Susan's bedroom was very near the top of the stairs. Their words and gasps echoed down the stairs to me and stayed in my ears all the time I ran across the road and into the woods. No matter how fast I ran, their voices stayed with me. I smelled creek water and deep damp forest shadow and the sweetness of pinecone. And then I came to a clearing, the sunlight suddenly blinding me, to the edge of Eagle's Point. I watched the big hawks wheel down the sky. I wanted them to carry me away to the world Edgar Rice Burroughs described in his books, where beautiful princesses and fabled cities and fabulous caches of gold awaited me, and people like me were never brokenhearted.

What I'd always suspected, and had always feared, was true: she loved David, not me.

I stayed till dark, smoking one Pall Mall after another, feeling the chill of the dying day seep into my bones, and watching the birds sail down the tumbling vermilion clouds and the silver slice of moon just now coming clear.

In the coming days, I avoided them, and of course they were full of questions and hurt looks when I said I didn't have time for them anymore.

Dad died the autumn I was sixteen, the concrete truck he was driving sliding off the road because of a flash flood and plunging a few hundred feet straight down into a ravine. Mom had to worry about the two younger ones, which meant getting a job as a checkout lady at Slocum's Market and leaving me to worry about myself. I didn't mind. Mom was only forty-six but looked sixty. Hers had not been an easy life, and she looked so worn and faded these days that I just kept hugging her so she wouldn't collapse on the floor.

I saw Susan and David at school, of course, but they'd months ago given up trying to woo me back. Besides, a strange thing had happened. Even though they lived on the wrong side of town and had the wrong sort of parents, the wealthy kids in the class had sort of adopted them. I suppose they saw in Susan and David the sort of potential they'd soon enough realize, first at the state university, where they both graduated with honors, and then at law school, where honors were theirs once again.

I stayed around the house after college, working the part-time jobs I could get, hoping to work full-time eventually at the General Mills plant eighteen miles to the north. I dropped by the personnel department there a couple of times a month, just so they'd know how enthusiastic I was about working for them.

But by the time they were ready to hire me, Uncle Sam he was downright insistent about having me. So they gave me an M-16 and a whole bunch of information about how to save your ass in case of emergency and then shipped me off with a few hundred other reluctant warriors and set us down in a place called Dan Tieng, from where we would be dispatched to our bunkers.

I've always wished I had some good war stories for the beer nights at the VFW and the Legion. But the truth is, I never did see anybody around me get killed, though I saw more than a few men being loaded into field hospitals and choppers; and so far as I know, I never killed anybody, either, though there was a guy from Kentucky I thought about fragging sometimes. I did not become an alcoholic, my respiratory system was not tainted by Agent Orange, I was not angry with those who elected not to go (I would not have gone, either, if I'd known how easy it was to slip through the net), and I never had any psychotic episodes, not even when I was drinking the Everclear that sometimes got passed around camp.

While I was there, Susan wrote me three times, each time telling me how heroic she thought I was, and how she and David both missed the old days when we'd all been good friends, and how she was recovering from a broken arm she got from falling down on the tennis court. Tennis, she said, had become a big thing in their lives. They'd both been accepted by a very prestigious old-line law firm and were both given privileges at the city's finest country club.

I wrote her back near the end of my tour in Nam, telling her that I'd decided to try golden California, the way so many Midwestern rubes do, and that I was planning on becoming a matinee idol and the husband of a rich and beautiful actress, ha ha. Her response, which I got a day before I left Nam, was that they were going to Jamaica for their vacation this year, where it would be nothing but "swimming swimming swimming." She also noted that they'd gotten married in a "teeny-tiny" civil ceremony a few weeks earlier. And that she'd been married in a "white dress and a black eye—clumsy me, I tripped against a door frame."

Well, I went to California, Long Beach, Laguna, San Pedro, Sherman Oaks . . . in three years, I lived five different places and held just about double that number of jobs. I tried real estate, stereo sales, management trainee at a seven-eleven, and limo driver at a funeral home, the latter lasting only three weeks. I'd had to help bury a four-year-old girl dead of brain cancer. I didn't have it in me ever to do that again.

By the time I got back to New Hope, Mom was in a nursing home equidistant between New Hope and Carstairs. I saw her three times a week. Back then, they weren't so certain about their Alzheimer's diagnoses. But that's what she had. Some days she knew me, some not. I only broke down once, pulling her to me and letting myself cry. But she had no idea of our history, no idea of our bond, so it was like holding a stranger from the street, all stiff and formal and empty.

I met and married Marcie, I got my job at the ambulance company, I joined the VFW and the Legion, I became an auxiliary deputy because my Uncle Clement was the assistant county sheriff and he told me it was a good thing to do, and I made the mistake of running into a cousin of Susan's one day and getting Susan's address from her.

The funny thing is, I was never unfaithful to Marcie, not physically anyway. I had a few chances, too, but even though I knew I didn't love my wife, I felt that I owed her my honor. Bad enough that she had to hold me knowing that I wanted to be holding Susan; I didn't have to humiliate her publicly as well.

I never did write Susan, but I did call her. And then she called me a couple of times. And over the next six, seven years, we must have talked a couple of dozen times. Marcie didn't know, and neither did David. She told me about her life, and I told her how crazy she was and where it would all lead, but she didn't listen. She loved David too much to be reasonable. I made all kinds of proposals, of course, how I'd just sit down with Marcie and tell her the truth, that Susan and I were finally going to get together, and how I'd give Marcie the house and the newer of the cars and every cent in the savings account. One time, Susan laughed gently, as if she was embarrassed for me, and said, "Earle, you don't understand how successful a trial lawyer David is. He makes more in a month than you do in a year." Then her laugh got bitter. "You couldn't afford me, sweetheart. You really couldn't."

There were a few more conversations. She saw a shrink, she saw a priest, she saw this real good friend of hers who'd gone through the same thing. She was going to leave, she had the strength and courage and determination to leave now, or so she claimed, but she never did leave. She never did.

The prison was a WPA project back in the Depression. Stone was carried from a nearby quarry for the walls. The prison sits on a hill, as if it is being shown to local boys and girls as a warning.

You pass through three different electronically controlled gates before you come to the visitors' parking lot.

You pass the manufacturing building where the cool blue of welding torches can be seen, and the prison laundry where harsh detergent can be smelled, and the cafeteria that is noisy with preparations for the night's meal. I walked quickly past all these areas. The rain was still coming down hard.

You pass through two more electronic gates before you reach the administrative offices.

The inmates all knew who I was. I wouldn't say that there was hostility in their eyes when they saw me, but there was a kind of hard curiosity, as if I were a riddle to be solved.

The warden's office had been designed to look like any other office. But it didn't quite make it. The metal office furniture was not only out of date, it was a little bit grim in its gray way. And the receptionist was a sure disappointment for males visiting the warden: he was a bald older guy with his prison-blue shirtsleeves rolled up to reveal several faded and vaguely obscene tattoos. He knew who I was.

"The warden's on the phone."

"I'll just sit here."

He nodded and went back to his typing on a word processor. He worked with two fingers, and he worked fast.

I looked through a law enforcement magazine while I sat there.

The receptionist said, "You do anything special to get ready?"

I shrugged. "Not really."

He went back to typing. I went back to reading.

After a time, he said, "It ever bother you?"

I sighed. "I suppose. Sometimes." I got into this five years ago when the state passed the capital punishment bill. MDs couldn't execute a man because of the Hippocratic oath. The state advertised for medical personnel. You had to take a lot of tests. I wondered if I could actually go through with it. The first couple times were rough. I just keep thinking of what the men had done. Most of them were animals. That helped a lot.

"It'd bother me." He went back to his typing again.

Then: "I mean, if you want my honest opinion, I think it'd bother most people."

I didn't respond, just watched him a moment, then went back to my magazine.

George Stabenow is a decent man always in a hurry. Pure unadulterated Type A.

He burst through his office door and said, "C'mon in. I'm running so late I can't believe it."

He was short, stout, and swathed in a brown three-piece suit. This was probably the kind of suit the press expected a proper warden to wear on a day like this.

He pointed to a chair, and I sat down.

"The frigging doctor had some sort of emergency,"

Stabenow said. "Can you believe it?"

"You getting another doctor?"

"No, no. But he won't be here for the run-through, which pisses me off. I mean, the run-through's critical for all of us."

I nodded. He was right.

He walked over to his window and looked out on the grounds surrounding the prison.

"You see them on your way in?"

"Uh-huh."

"More than usual."

"Uh-huh."

"Maybe a hundred of them. If it's not this, it's some other goddamned thing. The environment or something."

"Uh-huh."

"That priest—that monsignor—you should've heard him this afternoon." He grinned. "He was wailing and flailing like some goddamned TV minister. Man, what a jackoff that guy is."

He came back to his desk. To his right was one of those plastic cubes you put photos of your family in. He had a nice-looking wife and a nice-looking daughter. "You eat?"

"I had a sandwich before I left New Hope," I said.

"I'm going to grab something in the cafeteria."

I smiled. "The food's not as bad as the inmates say, huh?"

"Bad? Shit, it's a hell of a lot better than you and I ever got in the goddamned Army, I'll tell you that." He shook his head in disgust. "Food's the easiest target of all for these jerkoffs—to get the public upset about, I mean. The public sees all these bullshit prison movies and think, they're for real. You know, cockroaches and everything crawling around in the chili? Hell, the state inspector checks out our kitchens and our food just the way he does all the other institutions. Even if we *wanted* cockroaches in the chili—" He smiled.

"They wouldn't let us."

I said, "I need a badge."

"Oh, right."

He dug in his drawer and found me one and pushed it across his desk. I pinned it to my chambray shirt. The badge was "Highest Priority." All members of the team wear them.

"The rest of them here?"

"The team, you mean?"

"Uh-huh," I said.

"Everybody except the goddamned doc."

Before he could work up a lather again, I said, "Why don't I just walk over there, then, and say hi?"

"You've got twenty minutes yet. You sure you don't want a cup of coffee at least?"

"No, thanks."

He looked at me. "You know, I was kind of surprised that he requested you."

"Yeah."

"You sure you'll be all right?"

"I'll be all right."

"Some of the team, well, they had some doubts, too, said maybe it wasn't right. You knowing him and everything."

"I know. A couple of them called me."

"But I said, 'Hell, it's his decision. If he thinks he can handle it, let him.' Anyway, this is what the inmate wanted."

"I appreciate that."

"You're a pro, and pros do what they have to."

"Right."

He smiled. "I'm just glad Glen Wright has to handle the media. If it was up to me, I'd just tell them to go to hell."

He was going to upset himself again, and I wanted to get out of there before it happened. I stood up.

"You fellas used to carry little black bags," he said.

"Yeah."

"Just like doctors. Guess you don't need them anymore, huh? Now we provide everything."

"Right."

We shook hands, and I left.

There are six members on the team.

Five of us stood in the chamber and went through it all. You wouldn't think there'd be much to rehearse, but there is.

One of the men makes certain that the room is set up properly. We want to make sure that the curtains work, that's the first thing. When the press and the visitors come into the room outside the chamber, the curtains are drawn. Only when we're about to begin for real are the curtains drawn back.

Then the needles have to be checked. Sometimes you get a piston that doesn't work right, and that can play hell for everybody. They get three injections—the first to totally relax them, the second to paralyze them so they won't squirm around, and the third to kill them. In my training courses, I learned that only two things matter in this kind of work: to kill brain and heart function almost immediately. This way, the inmate doesn't suffer, and the witnesses don't get upset by how inhumane it might look otherwise.

After the needles are checked, the gurney is fixed into place. If it isn't anchored properly, a struggling guy might tear it free and make things even worse for himself.

Then we check the IV line and the EKG the doctor will use to determine heart death. Then we check the blade the doctor will use for the IV cutdown. We expose the inmate's vein so there's no chance of missing with the needle. That happened in Oregon. Took the man with the needle more than twenty minutes to find a vein. That wasn't pleasant for anybody.

Then I went through my little spiel to the man about to be executed. I'm always very polite. I tell him what he can expect and how it won't hurt in any way, especially if he cooperates. He generally has a few questions, and I always try to answer them. During all this, everybody else is rechecking the equipment, and Assistant Warden Wright is out there patiently taking questions from the press. The press is always looking for some way to discredit what we do. That's not paranoia, that's simple fact.

We didn't time the first run-through, which was kind of ragged. But the second run-through, Wright used his stopwatch.

We came in a little longer than we should have.

In the courses I took, the professor suggested that fifty-one minutes is the desired time for most executions by lethal injection. This is from walking into the chamber to the prisoner being declared legally dead by the presiding doctor.

We came in at fifty-nine minutes, and Wright, properly, said that we needed to pick things up a little. The longer you're in the chamber, he said, the more likely you are to make mistakes. And the more mistakes you make, the more the press gets on your back. Speed and efficiency were everything, Wright said. That's what my instructors always said, too.

Finally, I checked out my own needles, went through the motions of injecting fluids. My timing was off till the third run-through. I picked up the pace then, and everything went pretty well. We hit fifty-three minutes. We needed to shave two more minutes. We'd take a break and then come back for one more run-through.

When we wrapped up, Wright said we could all have coffee and rolls if we wanted. There was a small room off the chamber that was used only by prison personnel. The rest of the team went there. I walked down the hall to another electronic gate and told him that I was the man the warden called him about. Even though visiting hours were over, I was to be admitted to see the prisoner.

The guard opened the gate for me, then another guard led me down the hall, stopping at a door at the far shadowy end.

He opened the door, and I went inside.

The man was an impostor.

David Sawyer had gotten somebody to stand in for him at the execution. Last time I'd seen him was at the trial, years ago.

The sleek and handsome David Sawyer I remembered, the one with all the black curly hair that Susan had loved to run her fingers through, was gone. Had probably fled the country.

In his place was a balding, somewhat stoop-shouldered man with thick eyeglasses and a badly twitching left hand. He was dressed in gray prisoner clothing that only made his skin seem paler.

I must have struck him the same way, as an impostor, because at first he didn't seem to recognize me at all.

On the drive up, I tried to figure out how long it had been since I'd seen David Sawyer. Eighteen years, near as I could figure.

"Son of a bitch," he said. "You changed your mind. The warden didn't tell me that."

I guess what I'd expected was a frightened, depressed man eager to receive his first sedative so he wouldn't be aware of the next three hours. You saw guys like that.

But the old merry David was in the stride, in the quick embrace, in the standing-back and taking a look-at-you.

"You're a goddamned porker," he said. "How much weight have you put on?"

"Forty pounds," I said. "Or thereabouts."

He sensed that he might have hurt my feelings, so he slid right into his own shortcomings.

"Now you're supposed to say, 'What happened to your hair, asshole? And how come you're wearing trifocals? And how come you're all bent over like an old man?' C'mon, give me some shit. I can take it."

For a brief time there, he had me believing that his incongruous mood was for real. But as soon as he stopped talking, the fear was in his eyes. He glanced up at the wall clock three times in less than a minute.

And when he spoke, his voice was suddenly much quieter. "You pissed that I asked for you to do this?"

"More surprised than anything, David."

"You want some coffee? There's some over there."

"I'd appreciate that."

"You go sit down. I'll bring it over to you." Then the eyes went dreamy and faraway. "I was always like that at the parties we gave, Susan and I, I mean, and believe me, we gave some pissers. One night, we found the governor of this very state balling this stewardess in our walk-in closet. And I was always schlepping drinks back and forth, trying to make sure everybody was happy. I guess that's one problem with growing up the way we did—you never feel real secure about yourself. You always overdo the social bullshit so they'll like you more."

"You were pretty important. Full partner."

"That's what it said on the door," said the bald and stooped impostor. "But that's not what it said in here." He thumped his chest and looked almost intolerably sad for a moment, then went and got our coffee.

121

The first cup of coffee we spent catching up. I told him about Nam, and he told me about state capital politics and how one got ahead as a big-fee lawyer. Then we talked about New Hope, and I caught him up on some of the lives that interested him there.

We didn't get around to Susan for at least twenty minutes, and when we did, he jumped up and said, "I'll get us refills. But keep talking. I can hear you."

I'd just mentioned her name, and he was on his feet, going the opposite direction.

I suppose I didn't blame him. The courts had made him face what he'd done, now I was going to make him face it all over again.

"Did you know she used to write me sometimes?"

"You're kidding? When we were married?"

"Uh-huh."

He brought the coffee over, set down our cups. "You two weren't—"

I shook my head. "Strictly platonic. The way it'd always been with us. From her point of view, anyway. She was crazy about you, and she never got over it."

We didn't say anything for a time, just sat there with our respective memories, faded images without words, like a silent screen flickering with moments of our days.

"I always knew you never got over her," he said.

"No, I never did. That's why my wife left." I explained about that a little bit.

Then I said, "But I was pretty stupid. I didn't catch on for a long time."

"Catch on to what?" he said, peering at me from the glasses that made his eyes flit about like blue goldfish.

"All the 'accidents' she had. I didn't realize for a long time that it was you beating her up."

He sighed, stared off. "You can believe this or not," he said, "but I actually tried to get her to leave. Because I knew I couldn't stop myself."

"She loved you."

He put his head down. "The things I did to her—" He shook his head, then looked up. "You remember that day back on Eagle's Point when you almost pushed me off?"

"Yeah."

"You should've pushed me. You really should've. Then none of this would've happened." He put his head down again.

"You ever get help for your problem?" I said.

"No. Guess I was afraid it would leak out if I did. You know, some of those fucking shrinks tell their friends every-thing."

"I blame you for that, David."

His head was still down. He nodded. Then he looked up: "I had a lot of chicks on the side."

"That's what the DA said at the trial."

"She had a couple of men, too. I mean, don't sit there and think she was this saint."

"She wasn't a saint, David. She never claimed to be. And she probably wouldn't have slept with other men if you hadn't run around on her—and hadn't kept beating the shit out of her a couple of times a month."

He looked angry. "It was never that often," he said.

"Still."

"Yeah. Still." He got up and walked over to the window and looked out on the yard. The rain had brought a chill and early night. He said, "I've read where this doesn't always go so smooth."

"It'll go smooth tonight, David."

He stared out the window some more. He said, "You

believe in any kind of afterlife?"

"I try to; I want to."

"That doesn't sound real convincing."

"It's not the kind of thing you can be real sure about, David."

"What if you had to bet, percentage-wise, I mean?"

"Sixty-forty, I guess."

"That there *is* an afterlife?"

"Yeah. That there is an afterlife."

Thunder rumbled. Rain hissed.

He turned around and looked at me. "I loved her."

"You killed her, David."

"She could have walked out that door any time she wanted to."

I just stared at him a long time then and said, "She loved you, David. She always believed you'd stop beating her someday. She thought you'd change."

He started sobbing then.

You see that sometimes.

No warning, I mean. The guy just breaks.

He just stood there, this bald squinty impostor, and cried.

I went over and took his coffee cup from him so it wouldn't smash on the floor, and then I slid my arm around his shoulder and led him over to the chair.

I had to get back. The team had one more run-through scheduled before the actual execution.

I got him in the chair, and he looked up and me and said, "I'm scared, man. I'm so scared, I don't even have the strength to walk." He cried some more and put his hand out.

I didn't want to touch his hand because that would feel as if I were betraying Susan.

But he was crying pretty bad, and I thought Susan, being Susan, would have taken his hand at such a moment. Susan forgave people for things I never could.

I took his hand for maybe thirty seconds, and that seemed to calm him down a little.

He looked at me, his face tear-streaked, his eyes sad and scared at the same time, and he said, "You really should've pushed me off that day at Eagle's Point."

"I've got to get back now," I said.

"If you'd pushed me off, none of this would've happened, Earle."

I walked over to the door.

"I loved her," he said. "I want you to know that. I loved her."

I nodded and then left the room and walked down the hall and went back out into the night and the rain.

The next run-through went perfectly. We hit the fifty-one-minute mark right on the button. Just the way the textbook says we should.

Such a Good Girl

Nicole

Nicole Sanders went to the nurse's office during third hour and put on a pretty good imitation of a genteel seventeen-year-old girl down with the flu, genteel meaning a quiet, pretty girl who was still a virgin, had never tried drugs in any form, and read *Cousin Bette* for relaxation.

Of course, it helped that she was a good student (usually, a four point average), and generally perceived as a reliable girl. Nobody on the staff of Woodrow Wilson High School would suspect her of faking flu so she could get off from school. She had a near-perfect attendance record. She just wasn't the kind to lie.

But lie she did.

In the parking lot, she climbed into the sensible little forest green Toyota Gran had bought her for her seventeenth birthday last month. Gran was her best family friend now. Dad was off in California with his new wife. And Mom . . .

"I sure hate to see you come down with this stuff," the nurse said sweetly.

She headed home. This late in the morning, the expressway traffic was heavy. The sometimes foggy March rain didn't help, either.

Home was a nice Tudor in a small, upscale suburb of nice

Tudors and nice Spanish styles and nice multi-level moderns. Mom had gotten the house in the divorce settlement. Dad made a lot of money at his law firm and he'd inherited quite a bit when his father died several years earlier.

Nicole didn't stop at her house. She went down to the end of the block and parked behind a stand of pin oaks that was part of a small park-like area.

The cop-show phrase for what she was doing was "stake-out." She'd heard her mother call in sick this morning—she was a far better actress than Nicole and had put on a breath-taking performance—and now Nicole wanted to see what her mother did all day. As she'd passed by the house, she'd seen her mother's car in the drive. So Mom hadn't gone anywhere. Yet. And if Mom did go somewhere, Nicole had a terrible feeling that she knew where it would be . . .

Mitch

"I really think Mamet sold out. You know, when he went out to La-La-Land."

It was a good thing she had a lovely pair of breasts because otherwise Mitchell Carey would have kicked her ass out of the apartment as soon as he got done screwing her last night.

He'd picked her up at a cast party. A small theater group had put on an ancient Mamet one-act. It was the sort of theater group that attracted the worst kind of pretentious wannabes and the worst kind of cruising idle rich, the rich seeing theater groups (correctly) as being ripe with sex, drugs and just about any kind of octopus-like emotional entanglement a man or woman could want. It was from the idle rich, a few of whom were Mitch's customers, that he'd heard about the play; so, having made the club scene earlier in the evening, having played his role as the handsome, fortyish Jay

Gatsby to the disco and angel dust crowd, he decided to pop in on the theater folk. He'd stayed only long enough to meet Paula and woo her back to his den, whereupon he'd defiled her with great desperate pleasure. He hadn't merely screwed her, he'd ravished her and it had been wonderful. Three times they'd made love before heating up the remnants of a Domino's pizza lurking in his refrigerator. Then they'd found a great old Lawrence Tierney B-movie flick on a cable channel, "San Quentin," and only after it was over and they were back in bed again with the lights out, only then did she start talking about herself (age 39, born in Trenton, New Jersey, three husbands, worked as a street mime and part of a comedy group *a la* Second City, had in fact come here to Chicago to get *into* Second City but so far no luck, look at Jim Belushi, she said, only reason a no-talent like him ever got in was because of his brother and everybody knew it) but by then he'd put a finger in his ear and switched the HEARING button to Off. By the time she got to voicing her plans to audition for the revival of *Cat On A Hot Tin Roof* at the Ivanhoe ("I lose a little weight, and wear violet contact lenses like Liz Taylor, and learn how to talk Southern, I think I'd make a great Maggie The Cat, don't you?") he was blissfully asleep.

But now it was morning and she was standing naked at the sink in the bathroom while he was toweling off from his shower. And she was talking about how Mamet had sold out. Like Mamet would really give a shit about her opinion.

Then he noticed the time on the face of his Rolex that he'd set down on the tiny hutch next to the towel closet. He bought the best, man. Noticed the time and remembered his appointment. He had a customer he needed to meet at eleven-thirty. And it was now a quarter to eleven.

"I've got to hurry," he said. "I just remembered an appointment."

She was putting on her lipstick. She had remarkable lips.

"I hope we're going to do this again," she said, still drawing the blood tube across her mouth.

"Absolutely."

She glanced at him skeptically in the mirror. "For real?"

"For real."

"I hate bullshit promises. I'd rather have you say you won't be calling again than, you know, stringing me along."

"I'm not stringing you along."

"We did this Cole Porter show in Denver, you know? And anyway there was this guy and that's all he ever did. We spent one night humping like bunnies and the rest of the run, he'd call me to make a date an then call me back to break it. I guess I should be happy he at least *called* to tell me he was standing me up."

"You've sure had an interesting life."

She glanced at him in the mirror again to make sure that he wasn't putting her on. "Really?"

"Really."

She seemed satisfied. "You know, I wouldn't mind blowing you before we trundle off."

"That's all right. I really am late."

He could never figure out why he felt so good at night with them in the bed and so bad—and so sad—with them in the morning when they were getting ready to go.

What he needed was some kind of new kick. Ennui was the word he wanted. Ennui was what he was suffering from. He made a nice living, he got all the ass a reasonable man could want, and yet he was a little bored. Something new was what he needed.

But there wasn't any time for navel-contemplation this morning.

Had to hurry. He had an eleven-forty-five customer.

Kate

Thank God she'd been smart enough to take her watch along yesterday. Over noon, she'd hocked it. Place not far from the office where she worked in Lincoln Park. Guy with a glass eye and bad b.o. appraising both the watch and Kate herself. The watch he didn't have any problem with. Knew the exact market value. What he could pay out, what he could take in. The exact market value of the woman standing in front of him was another matter. Tall, elegant, beautiful in a nervous, vulnerable way. But going fast. Probably no more than forty-three, forty-four or so but going fast. He seemed to know why, too. Four-hundred, she got. Four-hundred.

Their house is shrinking. That's how she thinks of it. The last time after coming out of rehab and being a good little girl, the last time she fell off she hocked the TV, the stereo, the good china and the good silver. She'd had a good run. This was in the summer, Nicole visiting her father and his teenage-bride (Gwen is twenty-three, actually) for a month. Kate started hitting the clubs again, feeling good and young again. Sleeping around a little (always safe sex, of course), even developing a quick crush or two on younger men, the kind who used to be all over her, even when she was married, giving her ultra-conservative ex-husband one more reason to treat her like a whore. She could still remember the night a year into their marriage, that she'd told him about this little habit she had, which was where a lot of her household budget was going, and how he looked so dashed and doomed. It was almost comic, the way he looked right then, so shattered but self-righteous, too, as if it was impossible that anybody he'd even associate with could possibly be a junkie. A beautiful girl, the daughter of a powerful state senator, a Radcliffe grad, a suburban siren of stunning seductiveness, a coke head? There ensued eleven years—she had to give him that, he hung in there for eleven years—of one rehab program after another, trendy clinics and experimental programs all over the country. She'd gone as long as a year-and-a-half clean and sober, as they say. So much hope, so much anger, so much fear, so much despair, so much failure, hope-anger-fear-despair-failure, the same cycle over and over again. He never quite believed that she couldn't help herself. At least that was how she saw it. He never quite believed that she truly *tried* to kick once and for all. Poor sweet Nicole, she believed. That's why she was losing weight all the time and going into these terrible depressions (she'd been twelve when she took her first Prozac) and staying in her room practically every weekend when her mother was using. She could have joined her father in LA with his new bride but she feared for her mother, feared that if she went to California, her mother would die somehow. So she stayed. "You're such a good girl," her mother was always saying. Kate looked pretty good. The bones were the secret. She had good bones. Killer cheeks and a mouth that was erotic and just a wee bit petulant. Not enough to put men off. Just enough to intrigue. And the bod, even twelve pounds lighter than it should have been, the bod was good, too.

Four-hundred dollars in her purse and a day free of Mr. Cosgrove, her boss at the public relations agency, an egomaniacal twit who was always broadly hinting that she should go with him on one of his business trips east.

And on top of that, she would soon be seeing her old buddy Mitch Carrey.

Life was beautiful. Life was good.

Nicole

In the daylight hours, the jazz clubs and the art galleries and the odd little shops of Lincoln Park lost some of their nocturnal allure. A wild wailing sax sounded better carried on the wings of neon than on the gritty breezes of daytime. And crumbling brick facades had no romance to offer even the dullest of tourists.

Nicole followed her mother to a restaurant called The Left Banke, the intentional misspelling too clever by half. Good student Nicole knew that the original Left Bank in Paris, home to the cubists and the impressionists, not to mention Ernest Hemingway and Gertrude Stein, had probably been pretentious but at least had spared its tourists coy restaurant names.

Mom was driving the four-year-old Buick. The last time she'd gone off, she'd been forced to sell the Mercedes-Benz station wagon to make house payments. Nicole never told her father any of these things. She got tired of his sanctimony. Her mother suffered enough. At the meetings Nicole attended a few years ago, she learned that she was probably what the social workers called an enabler; i.e., she helped her mother keep up her habit. But what was the choice? What would happen to her mother if Nicole *didn't* help her? Easy enough for them to say let your mother hit bottom and find her own way back up. But what if the bottom was death? How could Nicole live with herself? She had tried everything to get her mother to stop. A year ago, she'd even cut her own wrists and been rushed to the hospital and put in the psychiatric clinic for three days of observation. Now, she was working on her own last, desperate plan, a way to force her mother to turn herself back into rehab and this time—Oh please God, please God, let it work for her this time—start on a life without cocaine. But first she had to find one thing out . . .

Her mother didn't get out of the Buick.

Just sat inside as the light rain started.

Slick new cars disgorged slick new people running in their Armani suits through the rain, laughing and swearing as they reached the canopied entrance.

And her mother just sat inside the Buick.

He drove an old red MG, the steering column on the right side. He wore a tweed jacket in honor of the MG. He even had a pipe stuck jauntily in the corner of his mouth. He looked like a soap opera's impression of a sensitive British novelist: dark, shaggy hair, and an angular face handsome but with a hint of cruelty in the eyes and mouth. He parked next to her mother and then quickly got of out the MG and hopped into the driver's side of the Buick.

Kate

"You look tired, Mrs. Sanders," Mitch said when he got in the Buick and looked over at her.

"I have a pusher who calls me 'Mrs. Sanders,' " Kate said, a touch of desperation in your voice. "Is my life fucked up or what?"

"You know," Mitch said, "this makes the third time I've had to warn you. And right now, with the rain and all, I'm in a pissy enough mood to just open this door and walk back to my car and not sell you anything at all."

"Oh, God," Kate said, genuinely scared. "I forgot. I used the P word, didn't I?"

"Yes, you did."

And he had indeed warned her before. About the P word. P for Pusher. He'd explained his circumstances. What he was: Mitchell Aaron Carey. What he hoped to be, with his looks and all, was an actor. And he'd tried hard for several years, too. All the humiliating auditions. All the even more humiliating little jobs around the various theaters (he'd actually scrubbed toilets at the Astor one weekend). Now he was just taking it easy. Doing "favors" for upscale people afraid of or put off by the usual array of street people who dealt drugs. How many pushers could give you twenty minutes on Aristotle's theory of drama? How many pushers had ever had a two-line part in a Woody Allen picture? How many pushers had Chagall prints hanging on their walls? He was no pusher. He was just an actor temporarily between gigs making a little jack on the side, and being very, very civilized about it.

"God, I'm sorry. I really am."

He smiled. "I guess I really don't feel like going back out into the rain right now."

"I brought the money."

"You're kind've strung out, huh?"

"Yeah. Yeah."

He was torturing her a little for having called him a pusher. "You thinking of maybe doing a line right here?"

"You wouldn't mind?"

He smiled again. "You're a good looking woman, Kate."

"Thank you." But it wasn't compliments she wanted. It was the stuff.

"In fact, I've been thinking about you a lot lately."

"You have?"

"Yeah," he said, and reached in the pocket of his stylish leather car coat. He took the stuff out and showed it to her. "Yeah. I've been thinking about you quite a bit lately."

Nicole

She followed him home. Watched him park. Watched him go up to his apartment. Then went into the vestibule and checked his name on the mailbox. The only male name on the four mailboxes.

She didn't feel quite ready for it yet. Tomorrow. She'd sleep on it. Sleep on it and think it through and kind of rough out how she'd approach him. Tomorrow was Saturday. No school. Tomorrow would be better.

When she walked in the house, her mother was dusting the living room and actually humming a song.

Nicole got tears in her eyes. This was her mother of long ago, before she'd discovered cocaine at a Los Angeles party ten years ago. She'd been there with her husband, visiting his relatives, and they'd ended up at a party in Malibu and she'd been drunk and up for just about anything—the party showing her just how much of her youth and adventurousness she'd had to give up as the wife of a neurosurgeon and so unbeknownst to Ken she'd tried it—and now she was happy only when she was stoned.

Dusting. And whistling. With the wonderful scent of a pot roast floating out of the kitchen.

She was Mom again. Nicole couldn't help herself. She flew to her and took her in her arms and suddenly they were both crying without a single word having been said, just holding each other. And then Mom said, "You're such a good girl, Nicole. And I love you so much."

Nicole didn't sleep well. She kept waking up and thinking about what she was going to say to Mitch Carey.

Her plan was simple. She would tell him that if he continued to sell her mother cocaine, she would turn him over to the police. She believed—hoped, was the more precise word—that if her mother was cut off from Mitch's supply, then she'd panic and turn herself back to rehab. And this time it would work. This time it *had* to work. Absolutely had to.

135

Carey would be pissed but what could he do? He certainly didn't want to go to jail.

Mom made pancakes for breakfast. Blueberry pancakes. The kind she'd made back when Nicole was a little girl, and Mom and Dad were happy.

"I guess I'll go study at the library," she said, after finishing breakfast and putting the dishes in the dishwasher.

"I'm going to do some more cleaning," Mom said. Then grinned. "It's kind of fun being a Stepford wife again. Now all I need is a Stepford husband."

Ninety-three minutes later, Nicole pulled her car into a slot behind Carey's apartment house. The interior stairs of the place smelled of rubber and paint. A new runner had been put on the steps and new paint on the walls. Whoever managed this place, they took care of it.

Carey answered the door out of breath and with a white nubby towel wrapped around his neck. He wore a tight white T-shirt and blue running shorts. A Stairmaster stood in the background. Classical music played. Carey had a strong, tight body.

"Yes?"

"I'm Nicole. Kate Sanders's daughter."

He looked surprised. "Is everything all right? Nothing happened to Kate did it?"

"No," Nicole said. "It's just that I'm thinking of turning you over to the police."

This time, he looked even more surprised. He grabbed her by the wrist and pulled her inside. "Hey, we don't have to invite the neighbors in on this, do we?" His nod indicated the three other apartment doors on this floor.

The apartment was impressive in a cold and calculated way. The furnishings were chrome and black leather, with a white and black tile floor and walls painted a brilliant flat white. The only touches of color belonged to the modernistic paintings on the walls. Nicole knew even less about painting than she did about classical music. This was the kind of room that intimidated her with her own ignorance.

Carey had quickly regained his composure. The panic and anger were gone from his eyes. He said, "Care for some wine?"

"No, thanks."

She had let two boys get their hands down her pants and play with her sex. At a ninth grade slumber party she had taken three drags on a joint. And she had looked at a couple of porno videos her Mom and Dad used to play when they thought she was upstairs asleep. This was the extent of her licentiousness. Drinking wine at this time of day was out of the question. Or any time of day. Wine always made her dizzy, and usually made her sick.

"Why don't you sit down over there on the couch and let me shut the machine off?"

He clipped off the Stairmaster and then wiped his face and neck again with the towel. He took the matching chair across from the couch. He sat on the edge. He kept pulling on both ends of the towel, biceps shaping as he did so. She knew this was for her benefit.

Hc said. "So you turn me over to the police, Nicole, and then what?"

"Then she gets so scared without her supply that she decides to try rehab again."

"I see."

"And this time she'll make it."

"So that's the plan, huh?" There was just a hint of a smirk on his mouth.

"That's the plan. I don't want you to sell her any more cocaine."

"What do I tell her when she calls?"

"Just tell her that you're not in the business any more. That you're scared of the police or something like that."

He looked at her and smiled. "If I ask you a question, will you answer it honestly?"

"If you'll turn down the music. It's pretty loud."

He was up and at the CD player in seconds. "Not a Debussy fan, eh?"

"Maybe some other time."

When he was seated again, he said, "Have you ever seen her happy when she wasn't doing coke?"

"Of course I have."

"I realize you think you're being honest. But think hard for a moment. And be honest with yourself."

She saw what he was getting at. Her mother was miserable when she was clean and sober. That, Nicole had to admit. She'd look at her mother and she'd look miserable. Tense, lost, angry, anxious. And late at night, she'd hear her mother sob. And there was almost never a smile. Or any expression of joy. Her life was simply a matter of *not* using cocaine. And she did not share the pride or the pleasure that others seemed to take in her *not* doing this.

His phone rang. "Think about it, kiddo." He reached over to a glass end table and picked up the phone. And said. "Hi. I've got company." He laughed. "Actually, yes, it *is* somebody you know. Your daughter." Then, "I take it you haven't told her." Pause. "Then that'll be *my* pleasure, I guess." Pause. "I'll call you in a while."

After hanging up, he said, "She said she hadn't had time to tell you yet. She wanted to wait for the right moment, I guess."

"Tell me what?"

"She's taking in a boarder."

"A what?"

"You know, a roomer."

"Who?"

He grinned. "Me. I'm going to be living with you for a while."

Mitch

In the first week, Nicole took all her meals in her room. She barely spoke to her mother, and she wouldn't speak to him at all. She spent several Friday and Saturday nights staying over at her friends' houses.

Mitch enjoyed the setup. He was tired of all the artistes and pretenders he'd hung out with the past ten years. It was enjoyable to get up in the morning and have a home-cooked meal and then spend a few hours "blocking out" a novel. That's what he called it, blocking out. Taking notes and filling up lined pages with blue ballpoint ink. Such and so would happen in Chapter Six, such and so would happen in Chapter Ten and so on. He liked to think he was editing a film, moving this scene from here to here. The writing itself, after all this preparation, was bound to be simple. Or so he told himself. Of course, in ten years, he'd actually never written a word of text. But what the hell. That really would be the easy part.

He stayed in a basement room that was fixed up for guests. He had his own bathroom and shower and TV set. He even had his own entrance, right on the side. His MG fit nicely into the third stall of the garage. He walked around the neighborhood on the sunny days. It was like being in a sitcom, all the neighbors tending their lawns and waving to him, the sounds of friendly dogs and driveway basketball, the aromas of backyard cookouts and fresh hung laundry on outdoor lines.

This was the change he needed. No doubt about it. He had

business to tend to but that took two, three hours at most a day. Had to keep his hungry little junkies hungry, and had to resupply his own stash with his own wholesaler. He always liked to tell people he was in retail, and so he was. This was the change he needed. A new kind of lifestyle. He felt invigorated, young.

He went easy on the sex, mostly for the sake of Nicole. If she found her mother in bed with him, she'd freak. Absolutely freak. She was a very pious little thing, sweet Nicole. Kate said she got the self-righteousness from her father. She said that was one reason she was so glad their marriage was over, so she didn't have him in her face all the time dispersing rules with a ferocity that would have put Moses to shame.

One rainy Saturday night, with Nicole sleeping over at a friend's house, he nailed her. She was as hungry for sex as she was cocaine. She was damned good: knowing, patient, clever and seemingly tireless. At one point, he rolled off the bed and lay on the floor laughing and screaming "Call 911! I can't take it any more!" And then she'd started laughing, too, and jumped off the bed, landing right on top of him. They spent an hour on the floor violating every silky hot orifice in her body.

He kept her coked up, and she kept him sexed up. At first, the first three-four weeks, they were discreet. Wouldn't want little Nicole to find out now, would we? They waited until she was gone before they did anything. There were a lot of nooners, Kate rushing home from the office for a line or two of coke and a ripping good time in the sack.

One night, when Nicole was upstairs in her room doing homework, they decided to do it in his room in the basement. It was like high school, the sneaking around, Nicole the stern repressed Midwestern parent, and them the fuck-happy teenagers. She didn't catch them. The next night and the next night and the next night and the next night, they did the same thing, Nicole working on her homework and them humping in the basement. God, it was great, and the danger made it just that much more delicious.

One Saturday afternoon, she caught them.

Nicole had come home early from the library, tired from a long day's studying. They didn't hear her. They were having too much fun in Kate's bedroom. But Nicole heard them. She flung the door open and stalked into the bedroom and went over to him and grabbed him by the long, dark hair. A handful came off in her grip. She pushed him off the bed and to the floor and shrieked, "I want you out of here! And I mean right now!"

Humiliated, enraged, Kate flew from the bed and slapped her daughter hard several times across the face, hard enough to draw blood.

Nicole spat at her, silver spittle hanging comically on the end of Kate's classical nose, and then stormed out of the bedroom, and out the house.

She didn't come home that night.

Kate started calling all her friends. None had seen her.

Mitch said that she was just punishing Kate, trying to scare her. Everything would be fine. He cooed, he cajoled, he caressed, and he finally got Kate back in bed. But the little bitch had spoiled his evening for him. Kate just wasn't there for him that night. Oh, they had sex all right, but there was none of her usual passion or ingenuity. It was like screwing a hooker who was having an off night. The little bitch really pissed him off. He was enjoying his suburban sojourn. He didn't want it ruined by all these mother-daughter politics.

She didn't come home until Monday after school. By then, even stoked up on coke, Kate was a nervous mess. Pacing. Biting her nails. Jumping every time the phone rang.

141

The little bitch.

She pulled in just as dusk was making it a better world.

She sat in her car in the garage a long time. Kate kept wanting to go out there. Mitch wouldn't let her. "That's what she wants you to do."

"I've been such a terrible mother to her, Mitch. I really have." She was begging him to let her go out to the garage. But by now, Mitch was genuinely resentful of the little prig. She resented him because he'd usurped her place as head of the family. Without him here, Nicole would be giving the orders. That's how it was in some junkie homes. The older kid took over and became the parent while the parent became a pathetic child. A power thing. Nicole had enjoyed the power. Now Mitch had the power. And he wasn't about to give it up.

She finally came in an hour later. She didn't say anything. Didn't even look at them. She just went straight up to her room and quietly closed her door. Kate spent the night fluttering around Nicole's door like a moth around a summer night's streetlight. But it did no good. Nicole wouldn't acknowledge her in any way.

Kate wouldn't come down to the basement, not this night or the next or the next. Kate pleaded with Nicole to speak to her. But Nicole came in the door at night and went straight to her room and reappeared only the next morning, in time to go to school. She wouldn't even say goodbye.

Mitch took it for a week, feeling helpless and sorry for himself. He did not like being at the mercy of the little bitch. She was spoiling his time with middle America. But Mitch, failed artist, failed husband, failed father, failed son, was nothing if not ingenious.

Mitch had a plan.

Nicole

She finally gave in, of course. Nicole.

Mitch was out somewhere. Mom was sitting in the kitchen. Drinking coffee. She looked great. The coke was killing her but it was a trade off. While she was dying, Kate looked better than she had in a long time, and was in a much better mood, too. Nicole poured herself a cup from Mr. Coffee and then came over and sat down at the kitchen table. The sunlight was bright and lazy in the air.

Neither of them said anything for a time. For this uneasy moment, they were strangers.

"You been all right, Nicole?"

"Yes. You?"

"This would be a very happy time for me if my daughter and I were getting along."

"Are you in love with him?"

Kate smiled. "God, no."

"But you sleep with him, anyway?"

"I *enjoy* him, honey. And part of that enjoyment is sex."

"And the drugs."

"Have you noticed how much happier I am? I mean, until you and I had our falling out?"

Nicole nodded.

"Have you noticed how much better I look?"

"I know what you're going to say, Mom. But you're wrong. The coke may make you feel better right now but it'll kill you eventually."

"Maybe that's not the worst thing, Nicole. To die, I mean. I enjoy the high, hon. I don't know how else to say it. When I'm high. I'm fine. And when I have my own pusher living right in my own home—" She smiled. "A junkie's dream."

"You shouldn't call yourself that, Mom."

143

"Well, that's what I am."

"You don't have to be."

"I'll never go back to another rehab program, Nicole. I don't want to be one of those zombies who just hangs on her whole life, trying to put off taking another line of coke. It's not a way to live. Especially since Mitch is right under my own roof."

"He doesn't care about you, Mom."

"And I don't care about him. Except that he keeps me happy with his drugs, and satisfied with his sex. You're old enough to understand that, Nicole."

"So I just live here with you?"

"You'll be leaving for college in California in four months. Then you won't have to worry about it any more." Then, "Don't you want me to be happy, Nicole?"

"You know I do."

"Then let me live the way I want to, hon. Then you can go away to college and not have to worry about me anymore."

"Oh, right. I go away to college and then I magically never worry about you anymore? It doesn't work that way, Mom. In case you hadn't noticed."

"Just be civil to him. That's all I ask. He doesn't like the way you and I are carrying on. Just be civil so he can enjoy himself while he's here."

Nicole carried her cup to the sink, washed it out, put it in the washer.

Then she went over and slid her arms around her mother and they hugged each other and they both cried and Kate said. "I just want to be happy and feel good for a little while, honey. That's all."

Nicole held her and kissed her. Tears filled her eyes.

A few minutes later, she was in her car and headed to the library. She had things to do.

★ ★ ★ ★ ★

Two nights later, the three of them ate dinner together at the long, mahogany table in the dining room. Candlelight, of course. Lasagna with fresh peaches and Caesar salad, Nicole's favorite meal, lovingly prepared by Kate after work. Dinner was late, but the food was delicious.

"How was school today?" Mitch said.

Nicole looked at her mother. Her mother looked frightened.

"Mitch, I'm going to try and get along with you for Mom's sake, all right? But don't pretend you're my father. Or that you're interested in my life. All right? I mean, that's really a pain in the ass."

Mitch laughed. "I hate to disappoint you. But I'm not *old* enough to be your father, Nicole. I'm only fourteen years older than you are."

"I thought you said you were thirty-nine," Kate said.

He patted her hand. "I only said that to make you feel more comfortable. I'm thirty-two."

"Maybe you're lying to make *Nicole* feel more comfortable," Kate said, not entirely pleased by this sudden turn in the conversation.

Mitch smiled. "Yes. Maybe I am."

And so it went. One week, two weeks. A family. That's what Kate pretended was happening, anyway. That the three of them were somehow bonding. Watching her like this made Nicole so sad she couldn't even cry. She'd just sit stunned for hours staring out the window of her bedroom at the dusk birds sailing down the salmon pink sky, arcing black shapes against the dying days, beings whose freedom Nicole could only envy.

Mitch

It was during Mitch's fourth week in the house that he cut Kate off. Unbeknownst to both Nicole and Kate, this was the plan he'd been working on for the past few weeks. He wanted to dominate his circumstances completely. And there was only one way to do that.

One afternoon, late, Kate came home from work tense and showing signs of needing her friend the white powder. Long day at work, the boss on her case, two of her coworkers in particularly grumpy moods. She related all this as she stripped out of her clothes and lay down on the bed with Mitch. Ordinarily, Mitch would have been right there with the coke. But not today.

When he didn't offer, she said, "I could really use a little boost, Mitch." That was her coy name for it. "Boost."

"You do for me, I do for you."

Her head had been on his naked chest. Now she rolled away from him and looked at his face. "Is something wrong?"

"You do for me, I do for you."

"I don't know what you're talking about." She was already getting a little shaky. "Please, Mitch, I don't mind playing games, but give me a little boost first, all right?"

He leaned over on an elbow and looked at her. "This is a good time for you, isn't it, Kate?"

"Yes. You know it is, Mitch."

"Me here. You getting a 'boost' whenever you need it. And the sex isn't bad, either."

"The sex is great."

"And you don't want it to end, do you?"

A flutter of fear in her eyes *and* her voice. "Don't want it to end? What're you *talking* about, Mitch? Why would it end?"

He hesitated. Went into one of his Acting 101 routines.

146

Looked down at the nubby bedspread, looked up at her briefly, then looked down at the nubby bedspread again. Troubled young man. Searching for the right words. Pure ham. But most of the ladies loved it. He said, in barely a whisper. "I'm going to ask you to do me a favor and you're going to get all pissed off and self-righteous and probably throw me out."

"I'd never throw you out, Mitch. God, I wouldn't, I wouldn't."

Impish grin. "That's because I haven't asked you my favor yet."

"Just ask me, Mitch. Just ask me."

So he asked her.

"Oh, Mitch." she said. "I should've known you were pulling one of your jokes on me. Get me all scared the way you did."

"It isn't a joke, Kate."

"C'mon, now, Mitch. I know how you like to put me on."

"No put on, Kate. I'm very serious."

"But you *can't* be serious."

But then she saw that he *was* serious.

And she got all pissed off and self-righteous and demanded that he leave the house right now. And for good.

A number of the neighbors commented on the screeching, dish-throwing, foul-mouthed argument that ensued within the walls of the Sanders place but that could be heard as far as half a block away. It went on like this, grand-opera style, for at least an hour. The neighbors hadn't heard arguments like that since the good doctor, her ex-husband, had moved out. Things must be going badly with her live-in.

Things must be going very badly.

Nicole

When Nicole got home that night, she found her mother at the kitchen table, her head down on her hands. Something was terribly wrong. She used to sense that when she was a little girl and her Dad was still living at home. She'd come home after school in the echoes of one of their arguments and her stomach would knot up and she'd feel alone and scared, scared that one of them might have killed the other, and she would start to shake and cry and say little prayers over and over again that everything would be all right.

A half-filled bottle of J&B scotch sat on the table in front of her. One glass. No ice.

Kate looked up at her wildly in the wan glow of the kitchen stove light. She was inching back toward her bag-woman demeanor, the hair wild and ratty, the eyes sunk deep and rimmed with black circles, the mouth slack with sparkling spittle collected in the corners. She'd been at work today. How had she accomplished all this just since work?

She was sitting in her bra and panties, with her long, lovely legs crossed. She was swinging her right foot to a rhythm only she could hear.

Nicole sat across from her. "Where's Mitch?"

"You're late."

"I was over at Sherry's."

"You should've called."

"I want to know what's going on."

"Nothing's going on."

"Bullshit, Mom. Bullshit."

Kate sighed. "I kicked him out."

"Why?"

"Because he's an asshole."

"That isn't an answer, Mom."

148

"It is for me. I kicked him out because he's an asshole. That sums it up pretty damned well, I think."

"You're shaking all over. He didn't give you a boost?"

"Screw his boost. I don't need his boost."

Mitch's words came back to her. About how happy her mother had been when everything was going well between her and Mitch. How he'd get all the boosts she wanted. How she kept herself looking great. How she was productive and happy. This was already like the old days. It was scary and sad. And not for the first time in her life did Nicole think of getting the gun out of her mother's dresser drawer and putting it in her mouth and killing herself. Many, many nights during the divorce, she'd thought of doing this.

"You want me to fix you something to eat?" Kate said.

Her words, her manner put a melancholy smile on Nicole's face. "Oh, yeah, Mom, you're in great shape to cook. One more drink of scotch and you'll pass out."

"And that's just what I *intend* to do, too. And don't you try to stop me."

Nicole sat there with her and watched her take one more drink. A good, big one. All the while muttering about how much better her life would be now that the asshole was out of it.

Nicole managed to get her to the downstairs john before she started throwing up. Then she managed to get her upstairs and in bed. Kate started snoring immediately. Nicole clipped the light off and went back to the kitchen.

She fixed herself a tuna sandwich on toast and had a few chips and a diet Pepsi. She cleaned up the kitchen and went to bed. But she didn't sleep. She wondered what had gone wrong with Mitch and her mother.

The deterioration was pretty fast. Nicole could remember

149

a time when it took her mother five or six days to get to the screaming, stomach-clutching, glass-smashing state in need of a boost.

This time, she made it in two days. She didn't go to work either one: the first day, she didn't even get out of bed.

Nicole missed another day of school.

She got in her car and drove over to a section where she was sure she could find plenty of drugs. She'd taken three hundred out of the ATM machine. She wasn't sure how much drugs cost but she figured that three hundred would be enough to buy *something*.

The trouble was that the street people scared her. She was always seeing TV new stories about car-jackings. Even with her doors locked, she didn't feel safe. She cruised the black streets but the angry curiosity of the faces—spoiled little white girl from the suburbs, what the fuck she doin' down here, fuckin' bitch—soon pushed her back onto the express-way.

She would have to convince her mother to go into the detox program run by one of the local hospitals.

But by the time she got back home, she found her mother drunk and belligerent. And the moment she brought up detox, her mother went into one of her violent frenzies.

Nicole stayed in her room all night.

The next morning, she called in sick to school and went to see Mitch.

He was using his Stairmaster again. Blue running shorts, white T-shirt. He didn't bother playing the suave host this time. He invited her in. He kept working out on the machine.

"Let me guess why you're here," he said. His tone was sardonic.

"You were right."

"I was? About what?" He was sweating and panting a little bit.

"My mother was very happy while you were there. The happiest I've seen her in a long, long time."

He smiled icily. "And you want me to come back."

"Yes."

He looked at her. "She tell you why I left?"

"No. Just that you'd had a fight. I thought maybe you'd tell me."

"I don't think so."

"I'd better let your mother tell you."

"I'm a big girl, Mitch. I can take it."

He smiled. "You go ask your mother."

"I want you to come back, Mitch. I'm sorry if I acted like a bitch. You made her happy."

He came off the machine so quickly, she was hardly aware of him at first. Sliding his arms around her back and waist, finding her mouth with his tongue, easing her against the wall so that she could feel his groin pressing against her.

She pushed against him but he was too strong. She tried bringing her knee up but he knew how to block it.

Finally, she bit his tongue. He fell back from her, cursing, dabbing his tongue with the tip of his finger. Then he laughed. "I knew you were a tough one, Nicole." He held up his finger. "Blood."

She walked to the door. Jerked it open. Walked out into the hallway. Slammed the door behind her.

When she came in the back door, she saw several empty glasses smashed on the floor. Mom had been on a rampage again, the need getting overwhelming.

She went upstairs. Sobbing sounds came from the large bedroom.

A weariness came over her. It was odd to be this young and yet be so worn out. She felt as if she were ninety. On the way over, she'd thought about Mitch grabbing her and kissing her. Then she'd thought about the argument Mitch and Mom had had. She had a pretty good idea now what it had been about.

She stood outside the door a long moment and listened to her mother cry. Only a few days ago, Mom had looked young and vital again. And was busy and productive. True, there were peaks and valleys in her mood and addiction level, but on balance life was good and happy again.

You couldn't beat having a live-in pusher, she thought.

She went into the bedroom. Kate peeked at her from behind a hand that lay against her face. "Go away. I don't want you to see me like this."

"I need to talk to you a minute, Mom."

"I can't talk now, honey. I'm sick. My whole body. Sick. You go downstairs or something."

"I think I know what you and Mitch were arguing about."

She sat down on the bed. Took her mother's hand. Held it to her own face. She could feel warm tears on the hand.

"I want to thank you, Mom."

"For what, hon?"

"For not asking me to do it."

Kate didn't say anything.

Nicole said, "He wanted me to sleep with him, didn't he?"

Kate didn't say anything.

"That's what you had the argument about, wasn't it?"

Kate didn't say anything.

"If I agreed to sleep with him, then he'd stay and keep you in drugs. That way, when he got bored with you, he'd sleep with me."

"He isn't a bad person, sweetie. He just looks at sex different from how we do."

"He's a creep. He took advantage of you and now he wants to take advantage of me." She kissed her mother's hand. "Thanks for not asking me to do it."

"I knew how you'd feel about it, honey."

"I appreciate it." She gently put her Mom's hand back on the bed and said, "Why don't I make you a little soup?"

"I don't know if I could hold it down."

"At least, let's give it a try." She hesitated. "Then I want to talk to you some more about rehab, Mom. You can't go on like this."

Kate looked beyond exhaustion. Something had died in her. The gleaming eyes, the happy voice of a few days ago were gone. "Maybe that's what I need. Rehab, I mean." She spoke in a dazed voice, staring tearily out the window. "Maybe I should quit fighting it."

"Why don't you take a little nap? I'll bring the soup up in a half hour or so."

Kate held her arms out. Nicole slid into her sleep-warm embrace.

Nicole was watching the MTV Top Ten countdown. Eight of the songs were rap, with sneering black guys pushing their faces into the camera. Nicole was too romantic for rap. She liked the ballads, especially by the black girl groups, who were as romantic as the boys were *un*romantic.

She yawned. She was exhausted and looking forward to bed. Three hours ago, she'd served her mother chicken soup and a glass of skim milk. She'd tucked her into bed and turned on the electric blanket. When Kate was in withdrawal, she got the chills bad.

She was just about to click off the TV with the remote when the gunshot exploded and echoed.

Her first impression was that something had blown up. Stove. Or water heater. Something like that.

But in the next moment, she realized what had really happened. Gunshot. The gun from Mom's drawer. Upstairs. Mom.

Fear blinded her.

She took the steps two at a time, tripping on the last of the stairway, grabbing the banister to keep from falling over.

Mom Mom Mom, she kept thinking.

The master bedroom was empty.

The smaller bedroom was empty.

She ran into the bathroom.

Her mother, completely naked, vomit covering her chest and stomach, her head twisted drunkenly to see Nicole, sat on the edge of the bathtub, a gun in her right hand. The top of her head was dusted with plaster from the hole in the ceiling that the bullet had made. A half-full bottle of J&B lay at her feet.

Nicole could never remember her this far gone. She stared at Nicole but with no recognition whatsoever showing in her eyes. Huge goosebumps covered her arms and legs. "No more fucking detox, kiddo," she said to no one in particular. "No more fucking detox."

She raised the gun to her temple. Or tried to. The movement was jerky and imprecise and gave Nicole plenty of time to grab her mother's wrist and ease the gun from her hand.

Then her mother began sobbing. She slipped to the floor, reeking of her own vomit and urine, wild-eyed and aggrieved beyond Nicole's imagining, slumped trembling and dry-heaving and crying on the pink bathroom rug.

Nicole knelt next to her mother but it did no good. Kate wrenched herself away. "I fucking hate you, you little snotty bitch! You want to put me back in rehab! I fucking hate you!"

Nicole tried several times to console her mother but finally gave up. Her mother had slipped into a fetal position and started muttering to herself in a language and cadence only she could understand. If even she could comprehend it.

Only a few days ago, this had been a happy woman.

Nicole slipped quietly from the bathroom, and went and made a phone call.

They were in the kitchen. Nicole and her mother. At the table. Drinking coffee. This was six hours after the shower incident. Kate had showered, eaten half a sandwich, and begun drinking black coffee as fast as Mr. Coffee could turn it out.

And, most important of all, Mitch had given her a boost.

Nicole had called Mitch. He'd agreed to come over. He'd brought a large suitcase. He'd agreed to try it again, with Kate and all, for a few days.

Mitch was upstairs now, in the master bedroom, waiting for Nicole.

"You don't have to do this, you know," Kate said. "You really don't."

"It was *my* decision, mother."

"I mean, you know how appreciative I am. And he *is* very good in bed, honey. And he promised me he'd be very, very gentle and take his time. You could do a lot worse, your first time."

"I'd better get up there. He's waiting."

"He's really not a bad guy, hon. He's really not." Then, "What're you going to wear?"

"Just my pajamas, I guess."

"Too bad you never liked sleeping gowns."

"I like sloppy old pajamas, Mom. They're comfortable to sleep in."

"You're so pretty." Kate touched her daughter's cheek. "And you're such a good girl."

Nicole looked upstairs. "Well, I'd better go."

She was just leaving the kitchen when her mother said, "You really don't have to do this, you know."

He was in bed. Propped up against the headboard. No shirt. Glass of wine. Cigarette going in the ashtray. A PBS concert of some kind on the tube. This was a very nicely appointed bedroom.

He smiled at her. "You looked scared, Nicole. I'm not the boogeyman. I'm really not."

"I'm not sure what I'm supposed to do."

He raised his wineglass. "Well, first of all, I want you to chill out a little. You know what I mean? Relax. Believe it or not, you just might enjoy this. Kate tells me you're a virgin. Is that true?"

"More or less."

"Oh-oh. Was there something you never told your mother?" The smile firmly in place.

"I've never gone all the way, if that makes me a virgin."

"Well, that certainly makes you a virgin in *my* book." He patted the bed next to him. "Why don't you come over and sit down next to me. I want you to like me, Nicole. I really do. We could have a very nice relationship. We really could."

"The three of us, you mean?"

"Sure, the three of us. Or just the two of us—and me—*and* the three of us. You and I would have one relationship, Kate and I would have another relationship. You see what I mean? And maybe sometime—" He paused.

"Maybe sometime what?"

"Oh, we'll talk about it later, maybe. For now, pour yourself some wine and sit down here and let's get to know each other a little better. All right?"

He was gentle.

A couple of times, she even found herself if not exactly enjoying it then not exactly *not* enjoying it.

She'd had all these preconceptions. That it would hurt a lot. That there would be a good deal of blood. That she would feel deeply changed by the experience.

None of these things happened to her.

They made love twice. They started on a third time but then he asked her gently if she'd mind doing him. The doing scared her more than the actual intercourse. She hated doing him and when she sensed he was going to come, she jerked him out of her mouth. She felt angry that he came all over her mother's bedspread.

He lay back and pulled her down to him, holding her. He lit a cigarette.

"So, do you hate me?"

"I don't want to talk about it."

"I tried to be gentle."

"You were gentle."

"I tried to be nice."

"You were nice."

"I was hoping you'd feel a little better about me, you know, after we'd done it and everything."

She said nothing.

"You hear what I said, Nicole?"

"I heard."

"So, do you feel any better about me?"

She said nothing.

"Guess you don't want to talk, huh?"

"I'd like to go to my own room now."

"Sure, if that's what you'd like." Then, "You know what *I'd* like?"

"What?"

"You remember when I said 'maybe sometime.' "

"Yes, I remember."

"Well, what I was thinking about was the three of us getting together all at the same time."

"My mom?"

"Yes."

"And me?"

"Uh-huh."

"Having sex with you?"

"It could be a lot of fun. I mean, I admit it sounds a little over-the-top at first. But when you think about it, it isn't all that raunchy. I mean I'm sure it's been done before."

She stood up. She felt sick.

It would probably happen, what he was talking about. Somehow they'd be able to convince her to get involved in it. Somehow.

"I'm going now."

"Just think about it, Nicole, all right? What I was talking about?"

She slipped out of the dark bedroom and went into her own bedroom.

In about half an hour, her mother came in. The bedroom was all shadow and silver moonlight. Nicole was under the covers.

"Nicole?"

No answer.

Her Mom came over and knelt next to the bed. "Did it go all right?" Nicole decided to answer. "Yes."

"Was he nice?"

"Yes."

"He didn't hurt you or anything?"

"No." Then, "Could we talk in the morning, Mom? I'm real tired."

She lay there for an hour trying to get to sleep. But all she could think of was what he'd suggested, about the three of them getting together.

She slept until late into the dark night. They woke her with their noises. Her first impression was that he was hurting Mom but then she realized it was just Mom's wild enjoyment she was hearing. Mom would go along with it when the time came. Not at first. Not without some convincing. But eventually, she'd go along.

She'd go along.

And so would Nicole.

Three different neighbors report the shots. People on the nice, quiet, respectable block are up from their beds and out the door, arriving in pajamas and nightgowns and robes and slippers just about the time the first patrol car reaches the Sanders' driveway.

A heavyset cop knocks on the front door of the Sanders's home, pauses, and then knocks again.

This is when the side door of the house, the one that opens on the driveway, eases open and Nicole appears.

None of the neighbors have ever seen Nicole look like this. Hair unkempt, pajamas torn and blood-soaked, hands filthy with blood. Blood everywhere. Even in her hair. Even on her feet. Blood. No mistaking what it is. Blood. She stands in the headlights of the police car, moths and gnats and mosquitoes thick around the headlights (big motor throbbing unevenly, needing points and plugs), and that is where the neighbors get their first good look at the knife she used. Butcher knife.

Long wooden handle. Good but not great steel. A knife she just grabbed from the silverware drawer before going upstairs.

A second prowl car. This one dispersing two cops. Man and woman. The man starts dealing with the crowd. Pushing them back. The woman goes directly to Nicole.

"I need to know your name, miss, and what happened here."

But Nicole is long gone.

The first cop comes down the steps. Says something to the female officer and then goes in the side door.

"What's your name, miss?" the female cop asks in a soft voice. "I want to help you. I really do."

The crowd has grown greatly in a few minutes. Two different TV stations are here now, one in a large van, the other in a muddy Plymouth station wagon.

The first cop is back from inside. Goes to the other male cop. "It's a mess in there. A man and woman. The woman looks like the girl there. She stabbed the hell out of them. It's a frigging mess."

A few people in the crowd are close enough to hear this. A whisper like an undulating snake works its way through the crowd. Shock and sadness and yet a glee and excitement, too. The shock for the pitiful young girl standing blood-soaked in the headlights, her mind obviously gone; and yet glee and excitement, too. Every day life is so—everyday. No denying the excitement here. And didn't Kate Sanders think she was at least a little bit better than everybody else? And exactly who was that man who'd moved in a while ago? And now look at Nicole. Poor, poor Nicole.

The reporter from the van, having heard what the cop found inside, now gets his cameraman to follow him around as he gets statements from various neighbors.

"Well, Kate, the mother, she and her husband split up a few years ago."

"They were very quiet people, really, though I think everybody knew that Kate had quite a few personal problems."

The cameraman angles his machine up the driveway, letting his lens linger on the lovely, crazed, blood-spattered girl standing in the headlights, Ophelia of the suburbs, which will make great fucking TV, just this lone shot of this lone heart-breaking crazy fucking girl.

And (voice over) a neighbor lady saying into the microphone: "It's just so hard to believe. She was such a good girl; such a good girl."

Aftermath

1

Not even the other cops much liked Frazier. He was too angry, too bitter to spend much time with. And he enjoyed the dirty aspects of the job too much. Hurting people. Shaking down shopkeepers and pushers and the richer variety of junkies. Getting freebies from the hookers and then beating them up afterwards and daring their pimps to do anything about it. In Vietnam, it had been called fragging, a grunt shooting his superior officer in the back and blaming it on the Cong. There'd been more than one boozy cop-bar conversation about good old Frazier getting fragged some night.

Josh Coburn managed to get the split pea soup off Lisa's face but not her white shirt. Oh well, what ten-month-old didn't walk around with part of her latest meal on her blouse?

"All right, honey," he said, down on one knee, steadying the home video camera so he could capture her walking toward him. "C'mon to Daddy."

Josh was babysitting his daughter tonight while Elise went shopping for their Christmas gifts. She'd laughed and said that Josh was more of a baby than Lisa about wanting to know what she was going to get them.

The living room of the Tudor-styled home sparkled with

decorations. This year's tree was so tall they'd had to cut off the top to fit the angel on. Blue, red, yellow and green lights played off the glass doors of the fireplace, and imbued everything in the room with an air of festivity.

"Daddy! Daddy!" Lisa giggled as she toddled toward Josh.

The camera was last year's Christmas gift. Elise had said that it was guaranteed idiot-proof, meaning that even a mechanical dunce like Josh could operate it.

And then he was on his feet, shooting straight down on her as she danced around in something resembling a circle, waving her tiny hand at Harold the Cat as he strode into the living room. "Hi Harral!" she shouted.

And then she was running toward Josh, arms spread wide. He swung her around and around. Daddy's girl. And neither of them would have it any other way.

He'd done this before.

It was an odd thought to have at this moment when her fists were smashing his face and her knee was trying to find his groin.

But she couldn't help but notice that for all the violence of his sudden assault, he was careful not to tear her clothes or bruise her. He was thinking of afterward. He did not want to mark up his victims.

And almost ludicrously—he was already wearing a condom. He'd probably put it on before he'd come to work. Ready. Knowing he was bound to run into somebody he could lure away as he'd lured her.

And then he was inside her. And she was sobbing. But she was no longer hitting him or trying to knee him. She was spent now. She just wanted it over with. She knew he wouldn't kill her. If that had been his intention, he wouldn't have been so careful not to mark her up.

He finished quickly and that gave her a strange surge of plea-

sure. He probably thought of himself as a swaggering macho man. And he couldn't even last two minutes.

Lisa wasn't old enough to say prayers. So there in her in pink crib, he said them for her. He prayed for Mommy and Daddy and Grandma and Grandpa and Harold the Cat and Princess her doll. Then he thanked God on her behalf for all the good things they had in their lives, and said a prayer for those who weren't so fortunate and asked that they be similarly blessed.

He gave her a kiss, checked her diapers a final time, and then turned out the light and left the room.

Downstairs, he fixed himself a light scotch and water and sat in the TV room watching the last of an NBA game. He kept the sound down so he could hear Lisa if she called out. He routinely checked her every fifteen minutes. He would have checked her every five but Elise had finally broken him of that neurotic habit.

Not until ten o'clock did he begin to worry. The malls were open an extra hour this last week leading up to Christmas. Maybe she'd stayed till ten. But if she had, why not call him? There were plenty of public phones around and she had a cell phone besides.

He thought of looking over the storyboards one more time. Early tomorrow morning they'd be pitching the Chuck Wagon fast food account. As the TV producer on the potential account, he'd be responsible for approximately a fourth of the whole dog-and-pony show. But, no. He'd looked them over three times earlier tonight. They were fine. He was proud of them. They were classic hard-sell ads and that's just what the account—which had lost 16% market share in the past two years—badly needed. Their present agency relied too much on whimsy. Chuck

Wagon needed a whole new approach.

At eleven o'clock, he was in Lisa's room, changing her. She'd developed a diaper rash and so he was powdering her when he heard Elise come in. He called downstairs to her but there was no answer. He wondered why not.

When he finished with Lisa, he rolled her on her back, kissed her forehead, and then went downstairs.

Elise was not in the kitchen. Or the living room. Or the bathroom. Or the den. Or the TV room.

And then he heard the faint noise from the basement. Elise was one of those women who liked instant contact when you came home. She always wanted a hug and kiss from you; and always returned the favor as soon as she got home. So why the basement? And why hadn't she responded when he'd called out to her from Lisa's room?

He opened the basement door. "Elise?"

No answer.

They had yet to finish the basement. It was a huge concrete bunker that housed furnace and washer and drier and assorted boxes with stuff they'd probably never use again.

He smelled gasoline. Smoke.

He rushed down the stairs so fast, he started to slide. He grabbed the slender wooden railing.

Elise stood, completely naked, in the center of the basement floor. Before her, in a pile, were the clothes she'd worn tonight. She'd set them on fire with the help of a small can of gasoline she'd apparently brought in from the garage.

She spoke only once. "I want you to go upstairs and not ask me any questions. Do you understand?"

The sensible, sensitive gaze of his good wife was gone, replaced by the kind of despair and frenzy one saw in the eyes of people who had just suffered some vast trauma.

"Elise. Please tell me what happened."

She shrieked at him. In the eight years of their marriage, the perfect suburban couple, she'd never once shrieked at him before. "Get out of here and leave me alone, you son-of-a-bitch!"

She'd never called him a name before, either.

There was nothing to say. Do.

He went doggedly up the stairs, like a man dragging himself to his own execution. What the hell was going on with her, anyway?

Four showers.

Twenty, thirty minutes apart.

Four different showers. What was she trying to scrub off her?

He lay in bed in the darkness, listening to the guest room shower down the hall. She didn't even want use their own shower. It was as if he'd alienated her in some irrevocable way. Every half-hour, he'd check on Lisa. He wanted to ask her what was going on with mommy.

He finally fell asleep near dawn.

Earl Frazier had made a bad mistake. It was one thing to rape hookers, as he sometimes did. It was another to rape women who lived in rich sub-divisions.

She was beautiful in a slender, almost ethereal way. But it hadn't been about sex . . . She was the kind of woman who'd snubbed him all his life. Who'd made him feel stupid and cheap and unmanly. She was so sleek and polished and perfect. He wanted to ruin that perfection for life. Feel his dirty hands ripping away her purity, her beauty, her money, her privilege.

But she would have access to power. And she could destroy him.

Why in God's name hadn't he been able to stop himself?

After his shift, he hung up his uniform neatly and lay in the shadows of his bedroom, sipping whiskey and smoking Pall Malls and praying—actually praying that God spare him this time. That he would never do it again. Whores, yes, because nobody cared about them. But not women of so-called virtue. That was just too damned risky.

Elise was in a white terrycloth robe and slippers when he came down for breakfast. The smells were good. Bacon, eggs, toast. This was much more than the usual mid-week breakfast.

One look at her and he knew not to ask any questions. He felt awkward, bursting with doubts and dreads and curiosity, but unable to give them voice.

He was just finishing up when she sat down across from him in the breakfast nook.

"Isn't your big presentation this morning?"

He nodded.

"I'm sorry. You probably didn't get much sleep and it's my fault." She started to put her hand out, to touch his, but then pulled it back abruptly. As if she'd suddenly recognized that touching him might contaminate her in some way.

He couldn't help himself any longer. "What the hell's going on, Elise?"

She said it simply. No dramatics. "I was raped last night."

"Raped? My God. Did you go to the police?"

She shook her head. "I couldn't."

"Why not?"

"It was a cop who raped me."

The Chuck Wagon presentation went pretty well. The two women in charge of the account from the client side laughed in all the right places and expressed enthusiastic interest in the coupon program the agency had come up with. The competition was killing Chuck Wagon with aggressive coupon programs.

Josh did well, too. It was one of those moments when a person stands aside and lets his doppelganger take over. Yes, it looks like me and sounds like me. But actually the real me is off somewhere else.

In this case, Josh was mentally stalking the cop who'd raped his wife. Josh did not embrace the adolescent beer-commercial machismo of so many advertising men. But he had a bad temper. And he also owned a .38 Special he'd bought at a gun show a few years ago. It was kept in the bedroom nightstand in case of prowlers.

All the way home on the freeway, he kept glowering at cop cars, wondering if this could be the one carrying Elise's rapist. Several times, he wished he had the family gun.

Elise left a note on the kitchen table.

TOOK TWO SLEEPING PILLS.
LISA NEXT DOOR. SHE'LL NEED
DINNER. LOVE, ELISE.

After retrieving Lisa from the neighbor's, Josh fed her dinner and then spread out some of her toys on the floor of the TV room. He tried to concentrate on the Seven O'Clock News but it was impossible. All he could think about was Elise being raped. He didn't kid himself. He knew that her pain and degradation were his main concern. Some women never psychologically recovered from being raped. But he also knew that his own ego was involved here. He felt that he'd failed her, hadn't sufficiently protected her, must now defend her after the fact.

He got Lisa to bed around nine. Around ten, Elise came down in a Northwestern sweatshirt—Northwestern being their mutual alma mater—and went into the kitchen and put on a pot of coffee.

They sat in the breakfast nook. All she'd had time to tell him this morning was that a cop had raped her. He'd had to hurry into the city and his pitch to the Chuck Wagon folks.

He said, "Tell me."

She said, "He pulled me over for speeding. I was out in the boonies. That new mall? I'd taken a wrong turn and was trying to get back to civilization. I was on some country road."

"He was a city cop?"

She nodded, sipping at her coffee. "He pulled me over for speeding. Told me to come back to his squad car and get in. I figured he was just going to give me a speech about my driving. Instead, he drove up the road to a grove of trees and then told me to get out of the car. He took me behind the trees and raped me." She looked tired but certain of herself. "That's all I'm going to say."

"Why didn't you report it?"

"God, Josh, are you forgetting Sandy Lewin?"

Sandy Lewin was a classmate of theirs. In their senior year, she'd been raped by a very trendy broker who'd earlier interviewed her for a job. By the time his lawyers got done with her, the impression had been left with the public at large that Sandy Lewin was a very sleazy young lady. Sandy was not only Elise's best friend, she was also one of the most respectable people Elise had ever known. But not anymore. Not to anybody who'd watched the rapist's lawyers destroy her on the Seven O'Clock News every night. Sandy had finally left town, relocated to LA. The broker went free.

"You have to report it, Elise."

"It's too late anyway. All those showers I took last night. I've destroyed the kind of evidence they'd need."

"You don't know that for sure."

She sighed. "I'm not going to the police, Josh. I couldn't

handle what Sandy went through." She stared at her coffee. "I wasn't exactly an angel in college, you know."

He'd met her when she was still trying to get over the senior who'd dumped her. She hadn't dealt well with her heartbreak. Drank, smoked, slept around. Had something of a reputation there for a while. The kind of thing defense lawyers get down on their knees every night and pray for.

"I don't want Lisa to ever have to hear about me that way. And if there was a trial, she'd eventually hear about it. About me. And this isn't exactly the kind of news Dad needs either."

Right now, her seventy-eight year old father's cancer was in remission. But news like that certainly couldn't be good for him.

He reached across the table and took her hand. She pulled it away as if he'd electrocuted her. "I love you so much, Elise. But to just let this thing go—"

"Now it'd just be my word against his."

They stared out at the night. It was just warm enough tonight for the raccoons to put in an appearance. He loved sitting here in the nook with the lights off, watching the raccoons play on the white snow in the blue moonlight. He liked it especially when the baby raccoons came along.

He said, "Do you remember what he looked like?"

"Sure."

"Do you remember any identifying marks?"

"No. But I remember the number of the squad car he was driving. Number 93."

"That's great."

"It is? For what? We're not going to do anything about it. So what's so great about remembering it?" She looked sad and weary. "I'll just have to work through this myself. Just please don't ask me any more questions about it."

The next two nights, Josh went looking for car 93. He had

an approximate sense of which precinct the car was from, and what part of the city it would be cruising.

He didn't spot it.

He came home late, exhausted, Elise asleep in the guestroom. She still didn't want to be in the same bed with him.

On his lunch hour, he walked to a nearby Barnes and Noble and found a book on the aftermath of rape.

Elise was following the general pattern the book outlined. Rage, shame, depression, anger, an inability to make any kind of physical connection even with her husband, even if that connection was as unchallenging as a hug.

There was one other terrifying piece in the book. One he'd already thought of because he'd heard it somewhere before. Some men, after their wives had been raped, blamed the women themselves. And no longer wanted to be intimate with them. The same way some men responded to their wives' having a mastectomy. Rationally, none of this made no sense. The women were the victims, not the men who loved them. But then given the male ego, he could see how some men might see the rape as some kind of abstract challenge to their own masculinity. He prayed to God that his male vanity never got that far out of control.

He was thinking of all this when, a few nights later, he spotted city police car number 93. The place was a strip mall. The police vehicle was parked in front of a shoe repair shop with a large front window. The car was empty. The cop was inside at the cash register.

Josh had pictured a hulking man. This one was tall but sinewy and slim. He was losing his hair. The way he was laughing with the shoe repairman, he looked like one of the many Officer Friendlys they had on TV to talk to kids. He was even just a tad nerdy.

When he came out and got in his car, Josh realized that he might be looking at the wrong man. Maybe the rapist was in another car tonight. Or it was his day off. Or he'd call in sick. He just couldn't imagine that this was the man. He picked up his cell phone and hit the proper speed-dial button.

"I know you don't want to talk about it, honey," he said. "I just want you to describe him for me."

"I thought we had an agreement."

"We do. I just want you to describe him."

"I thought you were at the office."

"I am."

"No, you're not. And you haven't been at the office the others nights either, have you?"

"Just please describe him?"

"Why?"

"I'm—working on something."

"Working on something? Just leave it alone, Josh! Leave it alone!"

"Just tell me if he's tall and slim and balding."

"Yes but—"

"I'll talk to you later."

He followed number 93 for nearly twenty minutes. He stayed a couple of cars back, the way detectives always do on TV. The .38 was in the glove department.

He didn't have any sort of plan. He'd just wanted to actually see the man. He'd told himself that that would be enough for him. But it hadn't been enough. Now he just wanted to follow him around. Hopefully, that would be enough.

But number 93 burst away from him suddenly, siren screaming. Probably a traffic accident somewhere. Or a tavern shooting. This was the kind of neighborhood for it, long, shabby, dying blocks.

At home, Elise accosted him as soon as he came through the kitchen door. "Where is it?"

"Where is what?"

"You know what I'm talking about. That gun you bought a year ago."

"Oh."

"God, Josh, that's all you've got to say is 'Oh?' Now where is it?"

"In my pocket."

"I want it. Now." She put her hand out, palm up. He put the gun in it. She slipped it into the pocket of her jeans. "If I can handle this whole thing, so can you."

Lisa started crying upstairs. Elise hurried to find out what was troubling her little girl.

After dinner, he thought of a good excuse to leave the house. He was low on computer supplies for his home machine. Office One was at a mall twenty miles away.

"You couldn't wait till Saturday?"

"I'm just going to the mall."

"I don't believe you."

"You've got the gun. What're you worried about?"

"You. That's what I'm worried about. Doing something crazy." She slid her arms around him. Pulled him close. "I know you love me, sweetheart. But it doesn't help me if I have to worry about you as well as deal with this thing myself."

"So he just gets away?"

"Sandy Lewin's rapist got away, too. And she got destroyed in the process."

"He'll do it again, you know. Rape somebody else. Maybe even kill them sometime."

"We have a life that I love. I'll learn to live with this. It'll take some time and some patience but if we really love each other we can put it behind us. I want another baby, Josh. And

I thought you did, too."

"You know I do. It's just the idea of him getting away—"

He kissed her more passionately than he had since she was raped. She surprised him by responding. No mad surge of passion. But her lips parted and she moved her hips gently against his. The mention of babies had brought back his favorite mental photo of her. There in the delivery room. Being shown Lisa for the first time. Thinking about it, he teared up.

"I love you so much," he said.

Office One was crowded for a weeknight. He bought more than $400 worth of supplies. He knew he should have gone straight home. Instead, he headed for the cross-town. And for the precinct where car 93 prowled the streets at night.

He found the squad car parked in front of a video store close to the strip mall where the cop had been the other night. He sat in the car looking into the store. He wished he would've found the cop in the XXX section. Instead he found him in the comedy section.

He was very conscious of the clock. He knew that if he was gone long, Elise would be suspicious. What was he doing here anyway? What good did it do to just follow the bastard around?

He put the car in gear and drove out of the video store lot.

He was seven blocks away when the emergency light bloomed blood red in his rearview mirror.

2

He pulled over to the curb. Waited for the cop to appear. A few cars went past, surveying the scene. Wondering what he'd done.

No swagger. Unassuming walk. Flipped open his ticket

book as he approached.

Josh had his window rolled down. The night smelled of distant rain and cold. It was in the low forties.

"Evening, sir."

"Evening."

"May I see your license?"

"Sure."

Showed him his license.

"The information here correct?"

"Yes; yes, it is." It was a good thing she'd taken the gun from him. He wanted to kill this man right here.

"Was I speeding, officer?"

"No."

"Taillight out or something?"

"One thing about a silver gray Saab. Brand new one."

"Oh? What's that?"

"There aren't very many of them."

"No, I don't suppose there are."

The cop handed him his license back. "Why're you following me, Mr. Madison?"

"Following you? You were behind *me*."

"The other night it was the shoe repair shop. Tonight it's the video store. And then you just follow me around in general sometimes. What's going on?"

"Gosh, I wish I knew what you were talking about."

For the first time he saw anger in the cop's face. "I catch you following me again, something bad could happen, Mr. Madison. You understand?"

Put the bullet right in the center of his throat. Watch the life choke out of him as he grabbed and clawed at the wound.

"You keep that in mind, Mr. Madison."

Josh woke up around two o'clock. A light rain haloed the streetlight outside. Elise was awake, too. They made love. He

175

surprised them both with the power of his ardor. He could have killed him. He knew now he was capable of it. It gave him new strength. He didn't tell Elise about seeing the cop.

Three weeks later, they were having after-dinner brandies in the TV room when Elise said, "My God, it's him."

Nine O'Clock News on WGN.

"Patrol officer Earl Frazier has been accused of rape by South Side resident Oreila McGee."

Frazier's photo was a color close-up taken some years ago.

"While McGee's lawyer, Jefferson Hardin, freely admits that his client is a prostitute, he insists that Officer Frazier beat and then raped his client this past Thursday night. Police spokesperson Donald Thomas said that the department will issue a statement tomorrow morning. But that as far as he knew, Officer Frazier would stay on his regular duty at full pay."

"Earl Frazier," Josh said. Now he knew the bastard's name.

"They'll laugh her out of court," Elise said, "a prostitute accusing a cop like that." Then, quietly, "He's just going to keep on doing it, isn't he?"

"Yeah," Josh said. "Yeah, he is."

"That poor woman," she said.

At breakfast, Lisa decided to decorate herself for the holidays. She got most of her Gerber's pureed carrots all over her face, hands, arms and hair. The carrots looked especially fetching dangling from her left ear lobe. She looked intensely, radiantly pleased with herself.

Josh fed her. He loved feeding her. "I think I'll run her through the car wash this morning," he said. "That'll clean her up." He'd almost cleaned out the small glass jar.

He glanced at Elise. She looked drained, tense. "You all right, honey?"

"I should've gone to the police that night. I should've told the truth. But it's way too late, now. It'd be just my word against his."

"Yours and a prostitute."

"God, I really want to see him in prison."

"So do I."

"But how can we do it now?"

He was glad that Lisa chose this moment to smear more of the carrot puree all over her face. "Gee, look, honey," he said, not answering her question. "An orange baby."

It was two days later when Josh got the idea.

He was in a TV studio producing a commercial for a car security system. Everything was wrapped up except the final sequence, which showed a shadowy burglar trying to break into a new Buick. The set was carefully lighted to effect a film *noir* look. The actor, dressed in dark clothes and a fedora, was hulking and ominous as he leaned into the car and glanced first right then left. Resembled a shot from a horror movie.

The sequence took on a more urgent meaning suddenly. He imagined that the burglar was actually Frazier the cop and that he was forcing Elise out of the Saab. He didn't want to imagine any more. He'd tried to avoid thinking of the actual rape itself. Doing so literally made him sick to his stomach.

"You all right?" the director said. They were in the control booth, a spaceship-like panel of knobs and buttons stretching out before them, Sixteen small monitors filled the dark wall in front of them. They could see the sequence being shot in both color and black and white. "Man, you're really sweating. Maybe you're getting that flu that's going around."

But it wasn't the flu. It was glimpses of the rape filling his mind. Her eyes. Her small fists hammering on him. The brutal way he'd taken her. And it was his idea. It had happened before, so why couldn't it happen again? An unseen private citizen with a home video camera out for a night's amusement when he accidentally stumbles on . . .

"Yeah," he said, finally answering the director. "Must be the flu."

Elise's first response was negative. She didn't think it would work. But the more he showed her the unedited video from the car security commercial, the more she got drawn in. There was a lot that needed to be done. And it wouldn't be cheap. He'd have to pay a lighting director, a camera operator, a makeup person, a costumer, two actors and an art director who could find the right car and fit it out accordingly.

The first night they were scheduled to shoot was canceled. Rain. The second night was also canceled. Fog. The third night, they actually got down to business. They drove out to the lonely, deserted spot where the rape had taken place and then everybody went about his job. They did every sequence over three or four times. He was afraid that reliving the experience would be too much for Elise. But her anger kept her sane. She'd been able to match the outfit she'd worn the night of the rape. She looked beautiful.

They didn't get home till midnight. Terri, the babysitter, was asleep on the couch, her senior History book over her face. Conan O'Brien was talking to her but she wasn't listening. Josh ran her home. By the time he got back, Elise was in the kitchen, micro-waving them hot cocoa with tiny bobbing marshmallows. They sat in the breakfast nook. She raised her cup. They toasted. Everything was ready to go.

Frazier had lived in an apartment complex ever since his divorce. He liked summers best because he had most of the day to hang around the swimming pool and size up the ladies. A lot of them were stewardesses. Being politically correct, the airlines had started using older women these days. The image of the vacuous but deadly-beautiful stew had changed. You now often found middle-aged ladies serving you on your flights. Still, there was plenty of young flesh around the pool, many of whom didn't mind coming over to his apartment for a gin and tonic and some after-noon delight. It was the cop thing. They'd deny it of course. But they—the type of women he attracted anyway—liked the authority thing. Even the women he raped. A few of his victims had even had an orgasm while he was raping them. Even against their will they'd responded to the uniform, the badge, the nightstick, the gun. One of them, he'd even used his nightstick on a little bit. He could still remember the way she'd shuddered.

He was still worried about the guy in the new Saab. Following him around like that. It was too late for the bitch to come forward with any evidence. So what was the use of following him around? The only answer was that the guy planned to kill him. Maybe he was just working up his nerve. He didn't look like the type who'd have the balls to do it face-on. He should never have raped the Coburn woman. He hadn't been able to control himself. Usually he stuck to the hookers. Stupid bitch that turned him in, she wasn't going to get anywhere. A hooker challenging a sworn officer of the law? Give me a break.

But the Coburn woman. What the hell was her husband fol-lowing him around for?

These were his thoughts the morning of the day the tape arrived. The mail came at one o'clock. Just after an argument with his mother. Bitch had cost him two marriages, the way she was always horning him. She'd never liked any of his girlfriends and absolutely detested his wives. His old man had dropped dead of a heart attack at forty-two. Frazier knew why, too. So he could escape. Whatever was on the other side of life—extinction or folks with wings or pitchforks—had to be preferable to life with his mother. He'd thought that moving away from her—leaving St. Louis and picking up his cop's life here in Chicago—would help. She was very tight with a dollar. She wouldn't let herself spend all that money on long distance. But she got in one of those cut-rate calling programs and now she was calling him all the time again. Sometimes, twice a day.

The first piece of mail he opened was a birthday card from his eight-year-old daughter. Today being his birthday. He smiled. She was his pride, his one true love. Carrie. She signed it with a big heart and a lot of XXXXs for kisses.

He knew something was wrong the moment he felt the video mailer. Just had some kind of foreboding.

Who'd be sending him a video?

He went upstairs and plugged it into the VCR.

And starting shaking immediately. Five minutes later, he was gunning down a couple drinks of bourbon and chewing on Tums. The tape—he couldn't see himself on it particularly well . . . shadowy and shot from the back . . . but you could see what he did to the woman grabbing her wrist the way he had that night . . . dragging her into the copse of trees. And then the camera moved in closer for a final shot of he and the woman disappearing into the woods . . . and held for a moment on the back fender of the squad car. Car 93. No doubt about that at all.

Josh called Frazier from a pay phone. All the afternoon traffic made for nice ambient sound. A blackmailer probably *would* call from a payphone.

"Good afternoon, Mr. Frazier." He tried to make his voice sound like a happy phone solicitor. After working with actors all these years, he had no trouble disguising his voice.

"Who's this?"

"A friend of yours." Pause.

"Yeah? What's your name?"

"What's more important is my occupation, Mr. Frazier. Or pre-occupation, I guess I should say. I spend most of my nights driving around and finding interesting things to shoot with my home video camera."

"Yeah? What's that got to do with me?"

"You're too modest, Mr. Frazier. You're the star of my last video. And my best, too, if I may say so. In fact, I think I remember sending you one."

He said nothing.

"It's a little out-of-focus, I'll admit. But you can see the number of the squad car pretty clearly. And you can see the woman pretty well, too. Sorry all we could see was your back. And that was pretty close up." They'd shot the sequence so that you could only see his shoulders and the back of his head. Jumpy, jerky shots, barely in focus. But ominous.

Silence. Then Frazier said, "We need to meet."

"All right."

"How about my apartment?"

"Fine."

"And alone. Tomorrow night at ten."

"You don't work then?"

"I'll worry about work. You just worry about yourself."

It happened more and more often these days. Private citizen with a home video camera. Roaming the night. Never knew where they were gonna show up. One had shown up the night of the rape. The son-of-a-bitch. Too late for the Madison woman to do anything. And the hooker's lawsuit wouldn't go anywhere. But a man with a videotape.

Frazier cursed himself again for ever letting go of himself this way. Nice, respectable woman. That was not the kind to rape and push around. He must've been crazy.

181

And the longer he thought of killing the video man right here in the apartment, that sounded crazy too.
There had to be a better way. Had to.

The store sold everything from guns to tiny microphones you could hide in a tiepin. It was the world of subterfuge and intrigue and it was fascinating to both Josh and Elise.

The chunky man with the crew cut and the American flag pin on the lapel of his sport jacket led them to what they were looking for. "They always make it look real complicated on cop shows. But actually it's pretty easy."

Elise laughed softly. "Can an idiot operate it?"

"An idiot can operate it fine," the salesman said.

"Then we're in good shape," she said.

At home, they spent two hours testing the equipment out. It operated simply, just the way the salesman had said it would.

Toward dinnertime, Elise took a nap with little Lisa. Josh used the time to go down in the basement and check over the .45 he'd bought a few days earlier. He'd known that eventually he would confront Frazier and he wanted to be ready. He was hoping the cop would force his hand. He very much wanted an excuse to kill Frazier. He took the .45 out to the Saab and put it in the glove compartment. He spent a moment looking at the decade-old black BMW Elise usually drove. It had been the first symbol of their success, of Josh moving from a small, factory-like art studio to one of the country's major advertising agencies. He'd drive it tonight. Frazier wouldn't recognize it.

He couldn't relax. He kept pacing in the basement. Thinking of Frazier. The Rape. The .45.

Finally, it was time to go. He went to the den and knocked back a drink of bourbon.

Elise watched him from the doorway. "Remember, you're not there to do anything more than we planned."

"I remember." But the harshness of his tone contracted his words.

She came over to him. Slid her arms around him. "This hasn't been easy for either of us, honey. I know that. I wish I could tell you when I'll feel like being intimate again but—"

He turned around and took her carefully in his arms. "All I care about is that you get better. That you come out of your shell. All the sleeping. Rarely leaving the house. Never calling your old friends—"

"Just don't do anything that makes things worse, Josh. You know your temper."

"Don't worry. Everything'll be fine. We'll nail the bastard. And I won't do anything stupid."

Then it was time to leave.

3

The parking lot of Frazier's apartment house told its own story. All the cars were wannabes, knock-offs of this or that sports car. Josh knew the place by reputation. The last bastion of middle-aged swingers. A number of divorced ad people lived here. A cop could do well for himself here. A certain kind of woman liked authority figures a lot.

He found the building he wanted and went inside, glad for a respite from the numbing cold. It was only a few degrees above zero and the clouds hiding the moon forebode more days of similar freezing.

Dance music filled the lobby from a nearby apartment. Some kind of updated disco number. It was a well-kept place. New carpeting recently vacuumed. Fresh paint. Window casings in good repair. He found Frazier's apartment and knocked. No answer.

Down the hall two fifty-year-old women emerged from
another apartment. They were nice-looking. They smiled at
him. "You're cute," one of them said. "You want to come
along?"

"Maybe some other time."

"You a cop, too?" the other one said.

"No, just a friend."

"Well, that story about him raping that hooker—he'll need
all the friends he can get. It's too bad when some old whore
can make trouble for a man like Frazier."

"He's very nice to everybody," the other one said.

"And—no offense—but some cops are pretty hard to deal
with. Especially after they've had a couple of drinks."

The other one giggled. "Remember Larry?"

Her friend returned the giggle. "After a couple of drinks,
he'd always haul out his bass guitar and take his pants off and
walk around in his boxers."

"I guess he thought he was turning us on," the lady
laughed. "Well, toodles, and if you see Frazier, tell him Kitty
and Candy said hi."

After they were gone, he knocked again. What the hell was
going on? Where was Frazier?

He tried knocking again. Then he started jiggling the
doorknob. A man came out of an apartment down the hall
and stared at him. Josh left.

In his car, starting the engine, he wondered what kind of
game Frazier was playing.

He drove away, preoccupied. He didn't notice, as he
reached the slippery nighttime street, that a blue Chevrolet
was following him.

The leak was slower than Frazier had figured. He'd slashed

Josh's right rear tire deeply. He'd also taken the spare. By now, the car should be limping along, giving Josh particular trouble on the ice-glazed streets. Trucks were out all over the city, spewing sand on the worst of the main-traveled streets. Cops had already given up on the idea of responding to fender-benders. There were just too many of them.

Then it happened quickly. The black BMW slumped to the right and the car started bumping toward a stoplight. He wouldn't be going much further on that tire.

He was beginning to lose it.

The tension of the whole situation. Frazier not being home. And now a flat tire.

He pulled the BMW over to the curb and pulled on the emergency lights. He got out of the car, slip-sliding on the ice, doing a couple of silent-movie arm-waving gags while he was at it. He walked back to the trunk.

Great. No spare.

He remembered passing a Sinclair station a few blocks back. There'd been a service garage as well as gas pumps.

Then he remembered the .45 in the glove compartment. He could lock the car but that wouldn't stop any real dedicated pro. They'd take everything, including the weapon. Better stick it in his pocket.

He got back in the car and opened the glove compartment and the gun wasn't there and he knew, of course, what had happened.

Elise had found it. Removed temptation from him.

He spoke a few nasty words to himself.

He was just getting out of the car when he saw Frazier standing there. Nobody had taken Frazier's gun. It was right in his gloved hand.

"Let's go back and get in my car," he said. "And be sure

185

and bring that videotape."

Josh glanced wildly around the street. Mercury vapor lights exposed a small convenience store, a tattoo parlor, a fingernail boutique, an ancient Catholic Church, three bars, a dry cleaners, a real estate office. The rest of the block, on both sides, were filthy giant houses that had long ago been divided up into filthy tiny sleeping rooms and so-called apartments. The legion of the lost plied these streets. Only the bars and the church had any succor to offer them.

Nobody was paying any attention at all to the two men standing by the downed BMW.

"You bring the tape?"

"Yeah."

"Let's see it."

Josh held up the videotape cartridge.

"Good. Let's get going."

Again, no swagger, no macho posturing on Frazier's part. He didn't have to impress anybody. He had a gun and Josh had no doubt he would use it.

"You drive," Frazier said.

Josh had to fight to control the car. It was a big, lumbering beast and tended to skid.

"The guy who took the home video, how much does he want?"

Josh almost smiled. Not only had Frazier bought the video as authentic, he was assuming that Josh was working with some nameless person who'd shot the footage. "Thirty-five thousand."

"I want to meet with him."

"I have the tape."

"You ever heard of copies?"

"He claims this is the original."

"I don't give a damn *what* he claims. I want to meet him.

But first I want you to go over on the Avenue and pull into where all those deserted warehouses are."

"For what?"

"Just do what I said."

Driving was still treacherous. They saw a couple of fender-benders on the way to the warehouses. Then Josh saw that the icy streets could help him. What if *he* plowed into a parked car? Maybe he'd have a chance to get away. It was his only hope.

"Slow down," Frazier said.

Josh saw an opportunity half a block ahead. A car just now pulling out. Perfect timing to ram into him. And in the confusion, run.

Then he felt cold steel against the side of his neck. "I'm not afraid to kill you, Coburn. Not at all. You try and pile us up, the first thing I do is put a bullet right in your heart."

Ten minutes later, Josh eased the car down a narrow alley between dark, looming warehouses. This had been a vital section of the shipping business until two large importer-exporters moved away. Now maybe as many as fifteen warehouses stood dark and empty.

"I still don't know what the hell you want with me," Josh said.

"Pull over there and kill the lights."

What choice did Josh have?

"Now kill the engine."

Josh switched off the key.

"The key."

Josh handed it over.

"Get out."

Josh was reduced to silent-movie sight gags again. He slipped and nearly fell on his back.

"I'm going to give you something to remember," Frazier

187

said. "And something for your wife to remember, too."

He drove his fist into Josh's stomach so hard, all time, all sensory data stopped. There was only pain. His entire body, his entire mind, his entire soul was pain. He wanted to scream, he wanted to throw up, he wanted to lash out at Frazier. But he was momentarily, and completely, immobilized. He just crouched in half there, his mouth open in a sound he didn't have strength enough to make.

Then the same fist smashed into the side of Josh's face. He remembered how, in *The Exorcist*, the girl's head had turned all the way around. Surely his head had just done the same thing.

"I don't want you or that bitch wife of yours botherin' me anymore, Coburn," Frazier said. "You understand me? We speaking the same language here?"

"You—you raped my wife," Josh managed to say. "I'll never stop bothering you."

"You ask her if she enjoyed it, Mr. Advertising Executive? You ask her how many times she came when I was inside her? Huh? You ask her that, you piece of shit?"

He started to move on Josh again.

And that was when the bullet tore through Frazier's left shoulder and he was turned leftward and slammed against the exterior wall of the warehouse next to him.

Moonlight shone on the ice-glazed tarmac of the warehouse area. Fog was setting in from the nearby Lake. The bullet had come from the fog. And now something else came from the fog, too. A familiar shape. Familiar except for the .45 she was holding.

"You try and hurt my husband again, I'll kill you right on the spot, Frazier," Elise said.

Josh was forcing himself past his pain so he could function again. Two of his ribs, his lungs and his head pounded with agony.

"You think you got it, honey?" Elise said.

"I was just afraid," Josh said, still out of breath, "when he hit me in the stomach he'd feel the wire."

"The wire?" Frazier said. "What the hell you talking about?"

"It's all been recorded," Josh said. "And it'll be on your commander's desk tomorrow."

Elise reached in and took Frazier's gun from him.

Then she moved a step closer and brought her knee straight up the middle of his crotch. He screamed and doubled over.

"That was for both of us," she said.

Then she led her hobbled husband away from Frazier and to the gray Saab parked three warehouses back.

Later, in bed, there in the sweet shadows, she said, "I'm sorry I still don't feel like it, honey. But I'm getting better all the time. If you can just hold out—"

He took her tenderly to him and kissed her. And gave her the answer they both wanted to hear.

189

Eye of the Beholder

1

All this started one spring when I couldn't find any women. The weather was so beautiful it just made me crazier. I'd lie on my bed in my little apartment feeling the moonbreezes and would ache, absolutely fucking ache, to be with a woman I cared about. I was in one of those periods when I needed to fall ridiculously in love. It wasn't just that the sex would be better—everything would be better. Fifty times a day I'd spot women who seemed like likely candidates—they'd be in supermarkets or video stores or walking along the river or getting into their cars. The first thing I did was inspect them quickly for wedding rings. A good number of them were unburdened. But still, meeting them was impossible. If you just walked up to them and introduced yourself, you'd probably look like a rapist. And if you told them how lonely you were, you might not look like a rapist but you'd sure seem pathetic. I tried all the usual places, the bars and the dance clubs and some of the splashier parties, but I didn't see it in their eyes. They were looking for quick sex or companionship while they tended broken hearts or simply a warm body at their dinner tables when too many lonely Saturday nights became intolerable—but they weren't looking for the same thing I was, some kind of spiritual redemption. Not that I didn't settle a few nights for quick sex and companionship, but next morning I felt just as lonely and disconsolate. But I couldn't settle very often. I wanted my ideal woman, this notion I've had in my mind since I was seven or eight years old, this ethereal Madonna I had longed for down the decades.

So of course the night I met Linda I wasn't even looking for anybody. I just walked into this little coffee shop over by the public library and there she was, sitting alone at the counter drinking coffee.

I wasn't sure she could rescue me, and I doubt she was sure I could rescue her, but at least the potential was there so two nights later we started going to bed and even though we were sort of awkward with each other, we kept trying until we got it right, and then we became pretty good lovers. The only thing that got me down was she was still pretty hung up on this football coach who'd dumped her recently. She kept telling me how it had only been for sex, and how he was an animal six, seven hours a night, which did not exactly fill me with self-confidence. I wasn't jealous of the guy but I didn't necessarily want to attend his testimonial dinner every night either.

The only thing that bothered me was her two teen-aged daughters. They were usually around the house while Linda and I were making love. Linda always laughed when I got uptight. "Hey, what do you think they do in their bedrooms when they bring their boyfriends over here?"

Linda was one of those modern parents. I'm not. My two kids, daughter and son, were raised pretty much the way I was: what your parents don't know won't hurt them. One boozy New Year's Eve I actually heard this teenage girl talking to her mother about how her tenth-grade boyfriend wasn't any good at oral sex. Linda wasn't that far gone but she was more liberal with her daughters than I would've been.

Even when my wife and I split up, we agreed that our kids would be raised properly, at least as we defined properly.

I kept wanting Linda to go to my place to make love but one night she laughed and said, "But your place is such a pit, Dwyer. I'm afraid I'd have cockroaches walking up my thigh."

Linda was three years divorced from a very prosperous insurance executive. She'd gotten the big house and the big car and the big monthly check. She only had to work part-time at a travel agency to make her monthly nut.

So we made love at her place and even though we both figured out pretty quickly that we weren't going to rescue each other, the thing we had was better than nothing and so we kept it up, even though I had a sense that she was vaguely ashamed of herself for liking me. Her previous boyfriends had run to doctors and shrinks and business executives. Security guard was a long way down the ladder.

Then one night I came over and she was late getting home from work. And that was the night it happened, with her sixteen-year-old daughter Susan, I mean.

Started out with an argument in the kitchen between Susan and Molly.

I was sitting in the living room watching a boxing rerun on ESPN. Linda had just called and said she was running late.

First I heard screaming. Then I hear cursing. Then I heard a cup or a glass being smashed against a wall. Then screaming again.

I run out there and find sixteen-year-old Susan slapping fifteen-year-old Molly across the face.

You have to understand, they were both extremely good-looking girls. But Molly was even more than extremely good-looking. She was probably the single most beautiful person I had ever seen, a Madonna with just a hint of the erotic in her dark and brooding eyes. Her sister Susan had always been jealous of her and now there was special trouble because Susan's boyfriend had developed this almost creepy fixation on Molly.

I got between them.

"Get the hell out of this kitchen," Susan said. "You don't even belong here."

"You shouldn't talk to him like that," Molly said.

"Why? Because our sweet mommy is fucking him?"

Molly shook her head, looked embarrassed, and left the kitchen. In moments, I heard her on the stairs, going up to the second floor.

Susan pushed past me and opened the refrigerator door. She took out a can of Bud, popped the tab and gunned some down.

"I'm sure you'll tell my mother I was drinking this." Before I could say anything, she said, "By the way, she's sleeping with this new guy Brad at the travel agency. That's why she's late. She's going to tell you all about it. But she doesn't want to hurt your feelings." She smiled at me. "On the other hand, I don't mind hurting your feelings at all."

"So your boyfriend dumped you, huh?" Hell, I was just as petty as she was.

For the first time, I felt sorry for her. The anger and arrogance were gone from her face suddenly. She just looked sad and lost and painfully young. She even lost some of the sexiness in that moment, tiny sad pink barrette turning her into a little girl again. She was all vulnerability now.

She went over to the breakfast nook and sat down in the booth.

"You want a beer, Dwyer?"

"You gonna tell your mom I took one?"

She laughed. "I actually like you."

"Yeah, I could tell."

"I'm sorry I told you about Mom's new boyfriend."

Women know all the secrets in the world. All the important ones, anyway. Men just know all that bullshit that doesn't matter in the long run.

"It was bound to happen," I said.

"You're not gonna be heartbroken?"

"For maybe a week. Or two. Probably more my pride than anything."

"He's sort of an asshole. I mean, I met him a couple of times. Real stuck on himself. But he's real cute."

"I'm happy for him. Maybe I'll take you up on that beer."

I felt betrayed, stunned, pissed, sad and slightly embarrassed. I was more of an interloper than ever in this house. Very soon now I'd be back to roaming my apartment and talking to imaginary women again.

I got a beer and sat down.

"You ever been in love?" she said.

"Sure."

"Really in love?"

"Uh-huh."

"It's terrible, isn't it?"

"Sometimes."

"This is the third one."

"Third one?"

"Yeah, the third boyfriend I've had who's fallen in love with Molly. The first one was in sixth grade. His name was Rick. I loved him so much I'd get the Neiman-Marcus catalogue down and look at wedding gowns. Then one day I found a note he'd written her. It took me a year to get over it." She shrugged. "Or maybe I've never gotten over it."

"So it happened again."

"Yeah. Paul—you met him—he broke off with me six weeks ago and he's been calling her ever since. She doesn't encourage him—I mean, it's not her fault—but he follows her around all the time. Takes pictures of her, too. He's the photographer for the high-school paper. Real good with a telephoto lens." She stared out the window. "He was like part of the family. Mom liked him, even. And she doesn't like many boys." She looked over at the sheepdog, Clarence, who was treated like the third child. Now he sprawled on the kitchen floor, watching her. "Clarence wouldn't bark at him or try to eat him or anything." Reference to Clarence made her smile.

"If it isn't Molly's fault, why'd you hit her?"

She shrugged. "Because I hate her. At least a part of me does. If she wasn't so beautiful—" She looked at me. "She's even got one of her teachers in love with her."

"Really?"

"Yeah. One day I was afraid my boyfriend was writing her letters, and so I snuck in her room and started looking around and there was this letter from Mr. Meacham, her English teacher. He said he loved her and was willing to leave his wife and daughter for her."

"Molly ever encourage him?"

She shook her head. "Molly is the most virginal person I know. Sometimes I think she's retarded. I really do. She's still a little girl in a lot of ways. She gets these crushes on her teachers. This year it's Mr. Meacham. He's teaching her the Romantic poets and Molly keeps telling me how much she thinks he looks like Matt Dillon, who's her favorite movie star. To her, it's all very innocent. But not to Mr. Meacham." She hesitated. "I even think she's started seeing him at nights. Last week I was out at Warner Mall and saw them sitting together in the Orange Julius."

"Does your mother know about this?"

"I haven't told her. She's got problems of her own with Molly. Well, with Brad."

"The guy at the travel agency?"

"Uh-huh. He's been over here a few times and it's pretty obvious he's fallen in love with Molly."

"You said he was young. How young?"

"Twenty-one."

"Well, that's better than Mr. Meacham lately."

"He may be the one stalking her."

"Someone's stalking her?"

"Yeah. Grabbed her the other night in the breezeway. But she got away. And been sending her threatening notes." She sighed. "I want to be pissed off at her but I can't. She doesn't understand the effect she has on men. She really doesn't." Then: "I feel like shit. God, I can't believe I slapped her. I'd better go talk to her."

"Good idea. Tell your mom something came up and I had to go."

"Sorry I broke the news to you that way. I mean, about Brad."

"It's all right."

"Like Mom says, I can be a bitch on wheels when I want to be."

We stood up and she gave me a hard little hug and then I went away. For good.

2

So it was back to the streets for me the rest of the summer. I kept thinking about Molly and how beautiful she was and how otherwise sensible men, young and older alike, seemed to take leave of their senses when they were around her. While I wasn't looking for virginal fifteen-year-olds, I was looking for the same kind of explosive love affair those men were, one that blinds you to all else, the narcotic that no amount of drugs could ever equal. In a few years, I'd be fifty. There weren't many such love affairs left for me. I'd had three or four of them in my lifetime, and I wanted one more before the darkness. So I went back to the bars, I became infatuated ten times a day in grocery stores and discount houses and even gas stations when I'd see the backside of a fetching lady bent slightly to put gas in her tank. But mostly my reality was my solitary bed and moonshadow, white curtains whipping ghostly in the rain-smelling wind, my lips silent with a thousand vows of undying love. A drinking buddy tried to make me believe that this was simply an advanced stage of horniness and I said it was, it was spiritual horniness and when I said spiritual he gave me a queer look, as if I'd told him that I'd started sending money to TV preachers or something.

The summer ground on. One of the investigators at Allied Security had to have a heart by-pass so they shifted me from security (which I like) to working divorce cases (which I hated). While I've committed my share of adultery, I can't say that it's ever pleasant to think about. Betrayal is not exactly a tribute to the human spirit. The men seemed to take a strange kind of pride in what they were doing. They didn't seem particularly concerned about being secretive, anyway. But the cheating women were all a little furtive and frantic and even sad, as if they were doing this against their will. Maybe they were paying back cheating husbands. Four weeks of this stuff before the investigator came back to Allied. My Advertising daughter came to town just as August was starting to punish us. My son drove in from med-school in the east. Their mother had married again, third time a charm or so she said, a man with some means apparently whom they liked much better than husband number two, a bank vice-president with great country club aspirations. "You've got to find yourself a woman," my daughter said right before she kissed me goodbye at the airport.

One night in late September, beautiful Indian summer, I came home and found Linda sitting in my living room.

"Your landlady let me in," she said. Then: "This is really a depressing place, Dwyer. You think we could go somewhere else?"

She didn't like any of the bars I recommended. Too downscale, presumably. We ended up in a place where businessmen yelled and whooped it up a lot about the Hawkeyes. The way they shouted and strutted around, you'd think they owned copper mines down in Brazil, where they could make people work for twenty-five cents an hour.

"Did you hear what happened to Molly? It was in the news about three weeks ago."

"I guess not."

"Somebody cut her up."

"Cut her up?"

"Slashed her cheeks. Do you remember a New York model that happened to a few years ago?"

"Yeah. She wasn't ever able to work again."

Linda's eyes glistened with tears. "The plastic surgeon said there's only so much he can do for Molly. She looks terrible."

"What're the police saying?"

She shook her head, sleek and sexy in a white linen suit, her dark hair recently cut short. "No leads."

"Molly didn't see her assailant?"

"It was dark. She parked her car in the garage and was just walking into the house—through the breezeway, you know—and he was waiting there. I guess this happened before—somebody in the breezeway I mean—but neither Molly or

Susan told me about it. Why should they tell me anything? I'm just their mother."

"She's sure it was a 'he'?"

"That's the assumption everybody's making. That it was a guy, I mean."

"She doesn't have any sense of who it might've been?"

Linda sighed. "Maybe."

"Maybe?"

She nodded. "I think she knows who it was but won't say."

"Why would she protect somebody?"

"I'm not sure." Pause. "I've been having terrible thoughts lately."

"Oh?"

"I've been thinking that Susan may have done this."

"Your daughter?"

"Yes." Pause. "She's very, very jealous of Molly. Molly—well, a few of Susan's boyfriends have fallen in love with Molly over the last year or so. About a month ago, Susan made up with this boy, Paul, the one who'd fallen in love with Molly. But then she came home one night and found Paul drunk in the living room putting the moves on Molly."

"You really think it's possible that Susan could do something like this?"

"She's been upstaged by Molly all her life. Even as a baby, Molly sort of unhinged people. I mean, she's the most beautiful girl I've ever seen. And I think I'm being objective about that."

"Anybody else who might have done it?"

"The police are talking to one of Molly's teachers, this Mr. Meacham. That's another thing my girls didn't tell me until after this happened. It seems this Mr. Meacham offered to leave his wife and daughter for Molly. He's forty-three-years-old. My God."

"Anybody else you can think of?"

After another drink was set down in front of her, she said, "I have to tell you something. It's so ridiculous, it pisses me off to even repeat it."

I just waited for her to say it.

"Last night, my dear sweet daughter Susan accused me of slashing Molly's face."

Calmly as I could, I said, "Why would she say something like that?"

"I'm kind of embarrassed telling you the rest."

"Maybe it'll make you feel better."

"I trashed Molly's room."

"When?"

"Late August, I guess."

"Why?"

"Brad."

"The guy from the travel agency?"

"Uh-huh. He'd started phoning her, Molly I mean, when I wasn't there. Then one night he came right out and asked me. I mean, I suspected something was wrong. He hadn't touched me in two weeks. Then this one night he said, 'Would it really piss you off if I asked Molly out?' I didn't want to let him know how pissed I was so I just said that I didn't think that was such a great idea but I said it in this real calm voice. I told him that technically she wouldn't reach the age of consent until October, and he said he'd wait. Then after he left—I sat in the den and got really drunk and then I went upstairs and started screaming at Molly, and then I started trashing her room."

She started crying, "My own daughter, and I treated her that way."

I changed the subject quickly. "You mentioned Susan's ex-boyfriend."

"Paul."

"Tell me about him."

"Right. He calls Molly four times a day. He says he doesn't care about her face being cut up. He loves her. His parents have called me, they're so worried about him. He went from A's to D's last semester. They want him to see a shrink. When Molly won't come to the phone, he gets furious."

"And you think Molly might know who did it?"

"I think so. Would you talk to her?"

"It'd probably be easier if you went through the agency. Ask them to assign me to you. I don't really have much time for any freelance on the side."

"Fine. I'll call them tomorrow. I really appreciate this, Jack." Then: "Oh God."

"What?"

"It's almost ten. I'm supposed to meet somebody at ten-fifteen way across town." She shrugged. "Met somebody new at the agency. He's a little older than Brad."

"Sixteen?"

She smiled. "Wise ass." Then: "I really am sorry. You know, about Brad and everything."

"I survived."

"I'd always be willing to see you again."

"I never take handouts except at Christmas time."

What the hell, it never hurts to sound dignified once in a while.

3

The next day, Linda led me up to the second floor den. "She sits in the dark. The blinds are drawn and everything, I mean. You'll get used to the shadows. She doesn't want anybody to see her. But I convinced her you only wanted to help her." Then she went away.

I knocked and a small voice said to come in and I went in and there she sat in a leather recliner by a TV set that was playing a soap opera. Just as I started to sit down in the chair facing her, a commercial came on, the bright colors flashing across the screen illuminating her face.

He'd done a damned good job. If it was a he. Long deep vertical gashes on both cheeks. The stitches were still on and that just made her look worse. But even with the stitches gone, her beauty would be forever and profoundly marred.

"Remember me?"

She looked at me with solemn eyes and nodded.

"You think we could turn the TV down a bit?"

She picked up the remote and took the volume down to a low number.

"Your mom wants me to make sure that you told the police everything, Molly. You understand that?"

Again she nodded. I had the unnerving sense that she'd also been struck mute.

"She told me what Susan said. About hearing somebody run away right after it happened, right?"

She said: "I wish I didn't have to go through this, Jack."

"I wish you didn't have to either, sweetheart."

"I mean your questions."

"Oh."

"My mom talked to the principal this morning. I'm going to finish my classes at home this year. So I don't have to see—anybody. You know, at school."

"You're going to sit in this room, huh?"

"Pretty much."

"With the blinds drawn."

"I like it when it's dark. When nobody can see me this way."

"Can I tell you about the breezeway, Molly?"

"The breezeway?"

"Uh-huh. I came out here last night and checked it out when everybody was asleep. You've got an alarm system that kicks on the yard lights whenever anybody approaches the house."

"I guess so."

"That means that when the person who did this to you ran off, you had a very good chance to see his face."

"Oh."

I waited for her to say more and when she didn't, I watched her for a moment—she wore an aqua blouse and jeans and white socks—and then I said, "I think you know who did this to you. And I think that you're trying to protect him."

"You keep saying 'him', Jack. Maybe it was a woman."

"Is that what you're telling me? That it was a woman?"

"No, but—"

"It'll come out eventually, Molly. One way or the other, the police are going to figure it out who did this to you."

"I just want it to be over with. I've accepted it and I just want it to be over with."

"It was either Paul or Mr. Meacham, wasn't it?"

"I don't want to talk anymore, Jack."

"Your mother loves you, Molly."

"I know."

"And she's very worried about you."

"I know that, too."

"She doesn't like the idea that whoever did this is still out there running around free."

"It's over with, Jack. It happened. And I don't have any choice but to accept it. People accept things all the time. There was a girl in my class two years ago who lost her legs in a tractor accident. She was staying on her uncle's farm. She'll never be able to walk again. People accept things all the time."

"He should have to pay for doing this, Molly. I don't know what's going through your head, but nothing justifies somebody doing this to you. Nothing."

I stood up.

"Susan is worried about you, too."

She nodded. "I'd like to watch this show now, if you don't mind." And smiled for the first time. Her scars were hideous in the flickering lights of the TV picture tube. "I appreciate you caring about me, Jack. You're a nice guy. You really are."

When I got downstairs, I found Susan and Clarence waiting for me. The big sheepdog lay next to the desk where Susan was working on her homework.

As always, the overtrained dog barked as I approached. I was going to get him some Thorazine for Christmas.

"Mom said to say goodbye. She had to run back to work." Then: "How'd it go with Molly?"

I told her about coming here last night and testing the yard lights. "She had to've gotten a good look at the person who did this."

"You're sure?"

"Positive. Tell me one more time. You were sitting in here watching TV—"

"—and I heard her scream and then I ran out to the breezeway and I saw somebody at the edge of the yard running away. He went up over the white fence out there."

"You said 'he'. Male?"

"I think so."

"And Molly was—"

"Molly was in a heap on the breezeway floor. When I flipped on the light, all I could see was blood. She was in pretty bad shape. Then Clarence came running out and he was barking like crazy." Then: "I think she knows. Who did it, I mean."

"So do I."

"But why would she protect him?"

"That's what I need to figure out. I'm going over to see our friend Paul."

"I'm trying to keep an open mind. The way he dumped me for Molly, I mean, I really hate him. But that doesn't mean he'd do something like this."

"No, I guess it doesn't." I leaned over and gave her a kiss on the forehead. "Anybody ever tell you what a nice young woman you are?"

"Yeah," she said. "Paul used to tell me that all the time. Before he fell in love with Molly."

4

Paul lived in a large Colonial house on a wide suburban street filled with little kids doing stunts on skateboards.

As soon as his mother learned who I was, her polite smile vanished. "You don't have any right to ask him any questions."

I was still outside the front door. "The family has asked me to talk to him."

"He didn't do it," she said. "I'll admit that he's been pretty involved with Molly lately. But he'd never hurt her. Ever. And that's just what we told the police."

She was a tall, slender woman in black slacks and a red button-down shirt. There was a kind of casual elegance to her movements, as if she might have long ago studied dance.

Behind her, a voice said: "It's all right, Mom. I'll talk to him."

Paul was taller than his mother but slender in the same

graceful way. There was a snub-nosed boyishness to the face that the dark eyes belied. There was age and anger in the eyes, as if he'd lived through a bitter experience lately and was not the better for it.

"You sure?" she said to Paul.

"Finish fixing dinner, Mom. I'll talk to him."

He wore a Notre Dame football jersey and ragged Levi cut-offs. His feet were bare. There was an arrogance about him, a certain dismissiveness in the gaze.

His mother gave me a last enigmatic look and then vanished from the doorway.

"I don't have much time," he said.

"I just have two questions."

"The police had a lot more than two."

"Can you account for your time the night Molly was cut up?"

"If I have to."

"Meaning what?"

"Meaning I mostly drove around to the usual places."

"And 'the usual places' would be what exactly?"

"The mall and the parking lot next to the Hardees out on First Avenue and then out to the mall again."

"And you can prove that?"

"Sure," he said. But for the first time his lie became obvious. His gaze evaded mine.

I said: "I saw her."

He didn't ask me who "her" was.

"When?"

"A few hours ago."

"Was she—"

"I didn't get a real good look at her. The room was pretty dark."

He surprised me, then, as human beings constantly do.

His eyes got wet with tears. "The poor kid."

"She's a nice girl."

"She's a lot more than nice."

"Susan's nice, too."

"Yeah, she is. And I treated her like shit and I'm sorry about it." He cleared tears from his voice. "I couldn't help— what I feel for Molly. It just happened."

"Molly's mother thinks you're obsessed with her. In the clinical sense, I mean."

"I love her. If that's being obsessed." He sounded a lot older and a lot wearier than he had just a few minutes ago.

"Her mother also thinks you were the one who cut her."

He smiled bitterly. "That's funny. I've been thinking it was her mother who did it."

"Are you serious?"

He nodded. "Hell, yes, I'm serious. Her mother's got a real problem with Molly. She's very jealous of her. Molly told me how bitter she was when this Brad started coming after her. She pushed Molly down the stairs, bruised her up pretty bad."

"She show you the bruises?"

"Yeah."

"She wasn't exaggerating?"

"Not at all."

Somewhere inside, a telephone rang, was picked up on the second ring. His mother called: "Telephone, Paul."

"Maybe I'd better get that."

"You can prove where you were when Molly was being cut?"

He surprised me again. "No, I can't, Mr. Dwyer. I can't. I was alone."

"How about the mall?"

He shrugged. "I just made it up."

"Then you were doing what?"

"Just driving around."

Mother: "Honey, somebody's waiting on the phone."

"Just driving around?"

"Thinking about her. Molly. I really have to go, Mr. Dwyer."

"Honey!" his mother called again.

5

This was the kind of neighborhood college professors always lived in in the movies of my youth, a couple blocks of brick Tudors set high up on the well-landscaped hills. The cars in the driveways ran to Volvos and Saabs, and the music, when you heard through the occasional open window, ran to Brahms and Mahler. At night, the professors would sit in front of the fireplace, blanket across their legs, reading Eliot or Frost. Even if life here wasn't really like this, it was nice to think that even a small part of our world could still be so enviably civilized.

A knock and the door opened almost at once. A heavy woman in a green sweater and a pair of too-snug jeans stood there watching me with obvious displeasure. She wore too much makeup on her fleshy, bitter face. Women who lived in these houses were supposed to look dignified, not like aging dance club babes. "Yes?" she said. Her mouth was small and bitter. She'd sucked on a lot of lemons, at least figurative ones, in her time.

"I'd like to see Bob Meacham."

She did something odd, then. She smiled with a kind of nasty pleasure. "Oh, God, you're another cop, aren't you?"

"Sort of."

I showed her my license.

"Well, come in, Mr. Dwyer. Would you like some coffee?"

"No, thanks."

I couldn't figure out why she was so happy to see me suddenly. Why would the presence of a private detective bring her such pleasure?

She flung an arm to a leather wingback chair that sat, comfortably, near a fireplace. An identical chair sat just across the way.

"I'll be right back."

She didn't go far. The floor creaked a few times and then she said, "So it's all over, is it, you bastard? Well, guess who's here to see you? Another cop. Your little girlfriend must think you were the one who cut her up."

When he appeared, moments later, he kept looking over his shoulder at his wife, as if waiting for her to put a knife in his back.

He came over and said, "I'm Bob Meacham."

"Jack Dwyer. Nice to meet you."

We shook hands.

"What can I do for you, Mr. Dwyer?"

"I wanted to ask you some questions about Molly."

"Oh. I see."

His wife, who stood to the side of him, smirked at me. "When we first got married, Mr. Dwyer, I used to worry that my husband was secretly gay. I guess I should be happy he just has this nice heterosexual thing for underage girls."

Meacham obliged her by blushing.

Seeing that she'd scored a direct hit, she said, "I'll go back to my woman's work now, and leave you two to discussing the wages of sin."

"I know what you must think of her," Meacham said softly as his wife left. "But it's my fault. I mean, I've made her like this. I've—I've had a lot of affairs over the years. We should've gotten divorced a long time ago but—somehow it's just never happened."

He didn't fit the professorial mould, either. He was a little too beefy and a little too rough in the face. He'd probably played football at some point in his life. Or boxed. His nose and jaw had the look of heavy contact with violence. He wore a chambray shirt and jeans. His balding head didn't make him look any more professorial, either. It just added to the impression of middle-aged toughness. He didn't belong in a Tudor house with a Volvo in the drive and T. S. Eliot lying open on his knee.

"You said you've had some affairs."

"Yes."

"Were they with young girls?"

"Youngish."

"Meaning?"

"Always of consenting age, if that's what you're getting at."

"Molly isn't of age."

"Molly's the first. A fluke. Being that young, I mean."

"You realize that hustling her has opened you up to several legal charges if the cops want to press them."

"You may not believe this, Mr. Dwyer, but I wasn't hustling her. We haven't slept together. I don't plan to sleep with her till we're married. I know people laugh at me, I mean I know I'm not much better than a dirty joke these days, but I don't give a damn about anything or anybody other than Molly."

He looked at me.

"You're smiling, Mr. Dwyer."

"Are you seeing a shrink?"

"No."

"You should be."

"I'm in love with her."

"She's fifteen."

"She's also the most spiritually beautiful creature I've ever known. That's why I say I'm not hustling her, Mr. Dwyer. That's why I say we won't make love till we're married."

"Or at least till he gets out of prison," Mrs. Meacham said, walking back into the room.

For the first time I saw the sorrow Meacham had hinted at. Saw it in the slump of her shoulder, saw it behind the pain and anger of her gaze. She looked old and sad and slightly adrift.

"He's going to lose his teaching job—the school is already seeing to that—and then the district attorney will charge him with contributing. He brought her over here one day while I was gone and they drank wine together. Isn't that sweet?"

She hovered at the back of his chair. The smirk back.

"He said he's going to leave me everything, when he runs away with her. Probably Tahiti, is what I'm thinking. He's always been obsessed with Gaugin. He even got sweet Molly interested in him."

She started wandering around the living room. We watched her with great glum interest.

"He's going to leave me everything, Mr. Dwyer. The mortgage. The car that has nearly 175,000 miles on it. The bank account that never gets above $2,000. And the cancer. I've had three cancer surgeries in the past four years, Mr. Dwyer. And I'll know in a few weeks if I need another one." This time there was no smirk, just grief in the eyes and mouth. "And you know the worst thing of all, Mr. Dwyer? I still love him. God, I'm just as sick as he is but I can't help it."

After a moment, Meacham said, "Why don't you go upstairs and lie down? You sound tired."

She looked at me. "I'm sorry for all this, Mr. Dwyer."

I didn't know what to say.

"That's why we don't have friends anymore. Nobody wants to come here and hear all this terrible bullshit we put each other through."

Then: "Goodbye, Mr. Dwyer."

After she left, he said, "I suppose you're getting a bad impression of me."

I almost laughed. He was pursuing a fifteen-year-old, cheating on his wife with cancer, and thinking of running away and leaving that same wife with all the bills. Gee, why would that give me a bad impression of him?

"My opinion doesn't matter."

He stared at me a long time. "I'm a romantic, Mr. Dwyer. I believe in the ideals of art and beauty. That's why I was so drawn to Molly. She's beautiful in an idealistic way—perfectly—a virgin of body and mind. That's why I want to take her away—to save her so that she doesn't become corrupted."

I thought of Brad dumping Linda for Molly; and Paul dumping Susan for Molly, and taking her picture all the time, and following her around obsessively; and I thought of how I'd been all summer, meeting perfectly fine women whom I rejected because they didn't fit my ideal. A dangerous thing, beauty. It brings out the best and the worst in men. The trouble is, sometimes the best and the worst are there at the same time—Meacham here loving Molly in the pure way of a college boy dumbstruck by the beauty of art; and yet at the same time willing to hurt a wife who was sick and needed him. The best and the worst. Beauty has a way of making us even more selfish than money does.

"She said no."

"Who said no?"

"Molly."

"She told you that, Mr. Dwyer?"

"In so many words."

"So you think that because she was taking some time to think it over—"

I sighed. "Meacham, listen to me. She wasn't thinking it over. There was no way she was ever going to run off with you. Ever. But maybe deep down you really understood that. And maybe deep down that's why you cut her face."

"My God, you really think I could do that?"

"I think it's possible. You're so obsessive about her that—"

" 'Obsessive.' That's a word my wife would use. A clinical word. There's nothing clinical in my feelings for Molly, believe me. They're pure passion. And I emphasize pure and passion. There's no way I could cut her up. She's the woman I've waited for all my life."

I wondered if I happened to be blushing at this point in the conversation. I thought again of all the women I'd stayed away from because they weren't my ideal. Good women. There's nothing like hearing your own sappy words put in the sappy mouth of someone else. Then you realize how inane your beliefs really are.

"Were you here the night it happened?"

"No, Mr. Dwyer, I wasn't. I was walking, actually."

"The entire night?"

"Most of it. You're wanting an alibi?"

"That would help."

"I don't have one—other than the fact that I'm a creator, Mr. Dwyer, not a destroyer. I have created something with Molly that is too beautiful for anybody to destroy. Even I couldn't destroy it if I wanted to."

I had to agree with his wife. I don't know why she stuck it out all these years, either.

"I'll be going now, Mr. Meacham."

A chill smile. "You don't like me much, do you, Mr. Dwyer?"

"Not much," I said.

"You're like her," he said, and nodded upwards to where his wife lay in her solitary bed. "Very middle-class and judgmental without understanding what you're judging."

"Maybe you're right," I said. "But I doubt it."

I left.

6

Clarence started barking at me the minute I pulled into the drive. He was in the breezeway, where he spent a lot of time on these unseasonably warm autumn evenings. Linda came out and calmed him down and let me in.

"I guess we should be grateful he barks so much, as a watch dog and all, but sometimes he drives me crazy." Then, apparently out of guilt for saying such a thing, she bent down and patted his head fondly, and said in baby talk, "You drive Mommy crazy, don't you, Clarence?"

Susan was in the kitchen setting out placemats on the breakfast nook table.

"We're doing Domino's tonight," Susan said. "Are you going to join us, Jack?"

I still couldn't imagine either of them doing it, cutting her up that way, daughter to one, sister to the other.

"Pepperoni and green pepper," Linda said.

"You convinced me."

Susan got beers for her mother and me and a Diet Pepsi for herself. Just as we were sitting down in the nook, Clarence exploded into barks again. The Domino's man had pulled into the drive.

"Maybe Clarence needs some tranquilizers," Susan said.

"I put a twenty on the counter there, hon," Linda said to her.

While Susan was out paying the pizza man, and calming Clarence, Linda said, "Did you talk to them?"

"Yes."

"Any impressions?"

"They're both good possibilities," I said. "Especially Meacham. I've been learning some things about him. He's a real creep. His wife has cancer and he's still running around on her. He thinks he's the last of the Romantic poets."

"Good for him. He's the one I'd bet on. For doing that to Molly, I mean."

Susan came back with the pizza and we ate.

Halfway through the feast, Linda said, "Tell him about Mark."

"Oh, Mom."

"Go on. Tell him."

Susan shot me a you-know-how-moms-are smile and said, "Mark Feldman asked me to the Homecoming dance."

"Great," I said.

"Honey, Dwyer doesn't know who Mark Feldman is. Tell him."

"He's a football player."

"Jeez, honey, you're not helping Dwyer at all. Mark Feldman just happens to be the best quarterback who ever played in this state. He's also a very nice looking boy. Much better looking than that creep Paul. And he's really got the hots for my cute little daughter here."

"God, Mom. The 'hots.' That sounds like something you'd get from a toilet seat."

We all laughed.

"Congratulations," I said.

"And she was worried that nobody'd want to ask her out anymore, Dwyer. Pretty crazy, huh?"

A knock on the breezeway door.

Susan went out to the breezeway to see who was there. She came back in carrying two pans.

"Bobbi brought your cake pans back, Mom. She said the upside down cake was great and thank you for the recipe, too."

"Thank Gold Medal flour," Linda said. "The recipe was on the back."

I guess it was the silence from the breezeway I noticed. Clarence tended to bark at strangers when they came up to the door and when they were leaving. But he hadn't barked at all with Bobbi.

"Why didn't Clarence bark just now?" I said.

"Oh, you mean with Bobbi?" Linda said.

"Right."

"He knows her real well. He doesn't bark with our best friends."

Then I remembered something that Susan had said to me back when I'd first met her.

I said, "He doesn't bark when Paul comes up, either, does he?"

"No," Susan said.

"The other night, when Molly was cut, you said you heard screams from the breezeway. But did you hear barking?"

Susan thought a moment. "No, I guess I didn't."

"Would Clarence have barked if Meacham had come up?"

"Absolutely," Linda said.

I tried not to make a big thing of it but they could see what I was thinking. I finished my three slices of pizza and my beer and then said I needed to go and do some work.

7

He wasn't too hard to find. I spent some time in the parking lot with some burglary tools I use on occasion, and then I went inside the mall looking for him.

He was hanging out with some other boys in front of a record store.

When he saw me, he started looking nervous. He whispered something to one of his friends.

Three good-sized boys stepped in front of him, like a shield, as I started approaching.

They were going to block me as he ran.

"Molly wants to see you," I said over the shoulders of the boys.

He had just started to turn, ready to make his run, when he heard me and angled his face back toward mine.

"What?"

"She wants to see you. She sent me to get you."

"Bullshit," he said.

I shrugged. "All right. I'll tell her you didn't want to come."

The boy in the middle, who went two-twenty easy, decided to have a little fun with the old man. He stepped right up to me and said, "You want to rumble, Pops?"

The other kids laughed. Nothing kids love more than bad dialogue from fifties movies.

"Like I said, Paul, I'll tell her you didn't want to see her." I looked down at the tough one and said, "If that's all right with you, Sonny."

I hadn't kicked the shit out of anybody for a long time but the tough one was giving me ideas.

"Fuck that 'Sonny' bullshit," the tough one said.

But Paul had a hand on his shoulder and was turning him back.

"She really wants to see me?"

"Yeah," I lied. "She does."

Paul looked at the tough one. "I better go, then, Michael."

"With this creep?" Michael said.

"Yeah."

Michael glowered at me. The others did, too, but Michael had done some graduate work in glowering so he was the most impressive.

"Nice friends," I said, as we turned back toward one of the exits. I said it loud enough to get Michael all worked up again. "Especially the dumb one with the big mouth."

We sat in an Orange Julius.

"I thought we were going to Molly's."

"We are."

"When?"

"Soon as you explain this."

From my pocket, I took a stained paper sack. "Know what this is, Paul?"

"You son-of-a-bitch."

"There's a hunting knife in there. A bloody one. I'll bet the blood is Molly's."

"You son-of-a-bitch."

"You said that already."

"That's illegal."

"What is?"

"Getting into my trunk that way."

"Wanna go call the cops?"

"You son-of-a-bitch."

"How about calling me a bastard for a while? Breaks the monotony."

"It isn't what you think."

"No? You ride around with a bloody knife in your trunk

and you don't have an alibi for the other night and it isn't what I think? You're telling me you didn't cut her?"

He started crying then, sitting right there in Orange Julius. He put his face in his hands and wept. People watched us. Son and father, they probably figured, with the father being a prime asshole for making his son cry this way. I took out my clean handkerchief and handed it over to him. I felt sorry for him. I shouldn't have but I did. Loving somebody can make you crazy. All the fine sane people in the mental health industry tell you you shouldn't give into it so hard but you can't help it. There was a poet named Charles Bukowski and he said that the most dangerous time to know any man is when he's been spurned in love. And from my years as a cop dealing with domestic abuse cases, Bukowski was absolutely right. So I sat there hating him for what he'd done to poor poor Molly, and feeling sorry for him too. He'd ended her life, now I was going to make sure that his life was ended too. He'd be tried as an adult and serve a long long sentence. The way all men who visit their rages on helpless women should be sentenced.

He started snuffling then and picked up my handkerchief and blew his nose and said, "You still don't understand, Dwyer."

"Understand what?"

"What really happened."

"Then tell me."

So he told me and I said, "Bullshit. I should beat your face in for even saying that."

"Let's go see Molly."

"Are you serious?"

"Absolutely."

I walked across to the payphones, keeping my eye on him all the time. It was preposterous, what he'd said.

When Linda came on, I told her I was bringing Paul over and taking him up to the den to see Molly. I said I couldn't answer her questions. She did not sound happy about that.

Soft silvered shadows played in the darkness of the den. Molly wore a pair of jeans and a white blouse and sat primly in the chair next to the dead TV. There was no question of turning on the lights. Molly had pretty much decided to live her life in darkness.

Paul and I sat on the edge of the narrow leather couch.

"He told me something crazy, Molly," I said. "I just wanted to give you the chance to tell me he's lying."

"I had to tell him, Molly," Paul said. "I'm sorry."

I told her what he'd said and she said, "Paul loves me."

"I guess I don't know what that means, Molly," I said gently. I was starting to get goosebumps because it appeared that Paul had told the truth, after all.

"He loves me. That's why he did it."

"Why he cut you up that way?"

"Yes."

"You wanted him to cut you?"

"I asked him to. He didn't want to. But I kept after him till he did it. I just couldn't take the way people acted around me. My face. It's why I was having all this trouble with my mother and my sister and my friends. I didn't ask for my face, Mr. Dwyer. I'd be much happier if I was plain because then I wouldn't have to have all these people after me like I was some sort of prize or something. I finally made him understand, didn't I, Paul?"

"Yes," Paul said.

"And he said he'd love me just as much if I didn't have my looks. And he does, don't you, Paul, even though I'll never be beautiful again?"

Even in moonshadow, his young face looked set and grim. He nodded.

Then she started sobbing and Paul went over to her and knelt next to her and took her in his arms and held her with a tenderness that moved and shook me. This wasn't puppy love or lust. This was real and simple and profound, the way his young arms held her young body. At that moment he was father and brother and priest and only coincidentally lover. I let myself out of the den and went downstairs.

8

"I'm having one, too," Susan said, when her mother asked her to bring us beers.

She brought three and we sat in the breakfast nook and I told them what had happened.

Linda cried and Susan held her.

"You think we should go up there, Jack?" Susan said as her mother wept in her arms.

"I'd give them a few more minutes."

"Do you think she's sane?" Susan said.

I shrugged. "I think she probably needs to see a shrink."

Linda sat up suddenly. She was angry. "That little prick took advantage of her. That's why he cut her face that way. He figured if he made her ugly nobody else would want her. He was just being selfish, that's why he did it."

She made a fist and muttered a curse beneath her breath.

"You think that's true, Jack?" Susan said.

"Maybe."

"Maybe he did it because he really loves her," Susan said.

"Maybe," I said.

"I'm not going to sit here and listen to that bullshit," Linda said. "I'm going up there."

And with that, she forced Susan out of the booth.

"Mother, maybe you'd better stay down here for a little while," Susan called.

"She's my god damned *daughter*," Linda said, sounding hysterical. "My god damned *daughter*."

She stormed off to the front of the house and the stairway.

Susan shook her head. "Maybe he really did do it because he loved her. Isn't that possible, Jack?"

She wanted to believe in love and romance, just the same way I wanted to believe in being redeemed by the right woman. There was a good chance we were foolish people. Maybe very foolish.

Then Linda was screaming and Molly was sobbing and a terrible rage and despair filled the house, like the scent of rain on a sudden chill black wind.

Susan said, "Could I hold your hand for a minute, Jack? For just a minute."

I did my best to smile but I don't think it was very good. Not very good at all.

"For just a minute," I said. "But not any longer."

Angie

Roy said, "He heard us last night."

Angie said, "Heard what?"

"Heard us talking about Gina."

"No, he didn't. He was asleep."

"That's what I thought. But I went back to the can one time and I saw his door was open and I looked in there and he was sittin' up in bed, wide awake. Listenin'."

"He probably'd just woken up."

"He heard us talkin'."

"How do you know?"

"I asked him," Roy said.

"Yeah? And what did he say?"

"He said he didn't."

"See, I told ya."

"Well, he was lyin'."

"How do you know?" she said.

"He's my son, ain't he? That's how I know. I could tell by his face."

"So what if he did hear?"

Roy looked at her, astonished. "So what if he did? He'll go to the cops."

"The cops? Roy, you're crazy. He's nine years old and he's your *son*."

"That little bastard don't give two turds about me, Angie. He was strictly a mama's boy. And now that he knows—"

He didn't need to say it. Angie had been waitressing at a truck stop when she'd met Roy. He was living in a trailer with his son, Jason, and his wife, Gina. He went for Angie immediately. On her nights off, he'd take her to Cedar Rapids, where they'd go to a couple of dance clubs. They always had a great time except when Roy got real drunk and started trouble with black guys who were dating white girls. Roy had some friends who were always talking about blowing up places with blacks and Jews and gays in them. Roy always gave them a certain percentage of his robbery money. That's what Roy did. He robbed banks, usually small-town ones that were located on the edge of town. Roy was a pro. He figured everything out carefully in advance. He knew the exit routes and where the bank kept the video surveillance cameras, and he checked out the teller windows in advance to see which clerk looked most vulnerable. He'd served six years in Fort Madison for sticking up a gas station when he was nineteen. He was thirty-six now and vowed never to be caught again. What she liked about him was that he had a goal in life. There was this one bank in Des Moines where he said he could get half a million on a payroll Friday. They'd go to Vegas and then they'd go see this whites-only compound up in the Utah mountains. That was the only part that Angie didn't like. She didn't understand politics and Roy and his buddies always carrying on about Jews and gays and colored people bored her. She had a way of looking awake when she was really *not* awake. She did that practically every time Roy and his buddies started talking about some militia deal they had heard about and intended to join.

The wife got wind of the courtship between Roy and Angie, though, and raised hell. She wouldn't give him a divorce, and she threatened to tell the cops about all his robberies all over the Midwest. So one rainy night he killed her.

Shoved a knife into her right breast, which silenced her, and then cut her throat. He loaded her into a body bag and packed a hundred pounds of hand weights in there with her and then drove his two-year-old Ford out to the river that very moonglow night and threw her in just below the dam. The only trouble Roy had was his son, Jason. The kid just kept wailin' and carryin' on about where's my mom, where's my mom? He hadn't wanted the kid in the first place, had beat the shit out of her, but she still wouldn't get an abortion. Even back then he'd had the dream of this big Des Moines bank on payroll Friday, and who wanted a kid along when you had all the cash with you? But Gina had her way and Roy was stuck with the little prick. And now Jason had overheard him talkin' about killin' his mother. Roy knew that somehow, some way, the little prick would turn him in.

Roy said, "Don't worry, I'll handle it."

She watched him carefully. "Sometimes you scare the shit out of me, Roy. You really do. He's your own flesh and blood."

"I didn't want him. *Gina* wanted him."

"And you killed Gina."

"For *you*," he said. "I killed her for *you*." Then, "Shit, honey, here we go again. Arguin'. This ain't what I want and it ain't what you want, either. You c'mere now." Then, "A kid like that, he's a ball and chain."

He liked it when she sat in his lap. He liked to feel her up to the point that his erection got so big and bulgy it was downright painful. She'd wriggle on it and make him even crazier. Then, as now, they'd go in on their big mussed sleepwarm bed and do the trick.

Afterward, today, he said, "I better get into town. I want to be there at noontime. See what the place is like around then."

He was scoping out a bank. He was planning to rob it day

after tomorrow. Their cash supply was way way down. The trailer park manager was on Roy's ass for back rent.

Roy said, "Don't say nothin' to him when he gets home from school."

"All right."

"You just let me handle everything."

"All right."

"It'll be better for us," Roy said, trying to make her feel better. "Haulin' that kid everywhere we go, that isn't the kind of life we want. We want to be free, babe. That's just the kind of people we are. Free."

Roy had killed people before and it had never bothered her. But never a kid before, that she knew of. And his *own* kid to boot.

He kissed her breasts a final time and then said, "I'll figure out what to do about Jason and then you'n me'll go dancin' tonight. Okay?"

"Okay, Roy."

Roy was gonna kill him for sure.

One day, when Angie was thirteen, her grandmother said, "That body of hers is gonna get her in trouble someday." The irony being that Grandmother herself had had a body just like it—killer breasts and hips that made young men weep in public—when she'd been young. And so had Angie's mother, the person Grandmother was talking to.

The thing being that the worst trouble Grandmother had ever gotten in was getting knocked up by a soldier home on leave from WW II, a pregnancy that had brought Angie's mother, Suzie, into the world. The worst Suzie had ever gotten into, in turn, was getting knocked up by a Vietnam soldier home on leave, a pregnancy that had brought *Angie* into the world.

Angie, however, got into a lot more trouble than just spreading her sweet young thighs. She saw a TV show one night where this beautiful girl was referred to as a "kept woman," a woman who lounged about an expensive apartment all day, looking just great, while this older man paid her rent, gave her endless numbers of gifts, and practically groveled every time the kept woman was even faintly displeased. An Iowa girl with a wondrous body like Angie's, was it any wonder she'd want to be a kept woman, too?

When she was fifteen, she ran away from home in the company of a thirty-two-year-old woman from Omaha who took her to a hotel in Des Moines. Angie slept with ten men in three years and made just over a thousand dollars. One of the men had been black, and that gave her some pause. She could just hear her dad if he ever found out about her (A) screwing men for money or (B) screwing a *black man* for money.

She went back home. Her dad, who worked as an appliance service repair man for Al's American Appliances, didn't have the money for a private shrink so they sent her to the county Human Services Department, where she saw this counselor for free. She spent two hours filling out the Minnesota Multiphasic Personality Test, which just about bored her ass off. He kept peeking in the room and asking her if she was about done. That's what he *pretended* to do, anyway. What he was really doing was staring at her breasts. He'd fallen in love with them the moment they walked in the door. She ended up screwing him on the side. He had a wife who worked at Wal-Mart in Cedar Rapids and two little girls, one of whom was lame in some way and whom he got all sad about sometimes. He was thirty-eight and bald and felt guilty about screwing her and cheating on his wife and all but he said that her tits just made him dizzy when he touched them, just dizzy. He kept her in rap CDs. She loved rap. The way the gangsters in the rap videos took care of their girlfriends. That's what she wanted. She wanted to meet some guy who'd give her a life of ease. A kept woman. No work. No hassle. No sweat. Just sit around some fancy apartment and read comic books and watch MTV and porno movies. She loved porno movies. The thing was, she didn't like sex very much, except for masturbating, but if sex was the price she had to pay for a life of ease, so be it.

She dropped the counselor as soon as she managed to get through high school. She got a job in Cedar Rapids as a clerk in a Target store. She lasted three weeks. She took her paycheck and bought a very sexy dress and then she started hanging out in the lawyer bars downtown. Her first couple of months, things went pretty good. She hadn't found a guy who'd make her an official kept woman, but she'd found several guys who'd give her a little money now and then, enough money for a nice little apartment and a six-year-old Oldsmobile.

But things did not go well after a time. She caught the clap and profoundly displeased a couple of the men who gave her money. Then she ran into two men who were long of tongue but short of wallet, a car salesman who drove them around in sleek new Caddies, and a supper club owner who wore her like a pinkie ring. They were full of promises but had no real money. The Caddie man had two wives and two alimonies; and the supper club man owed the IRS boys so much in back taxes, he could barely afford a pack of gum. He'd had a supper club over in Rock Island several years back, and he'd been charged with tax evasion, later dropped to a simple (if overwhelming) tax debt.

Then, the worst thing of all happened. On the night of her twenty-sixth birthday, Angie got busted for prostitution. She was in a downtown bar sitting with a couple of hookers she knew getting birthday party drunk, when one of the lawyers suggested they all go out to his houseboat. Well, they did, and the cops followed them. Angie insisted that she accepted gifts but never cash for sex per se but it was a distinction apparently too subtle for the minds of the gendarmes. They hated these two particular lawyers and were gleeful about arresting them. Cedar Rapids had a new police station and Angie was impressed with it. She saw a couple of cute young cops, too, and thought she wouldn't mind dating a cop. It was probably fun. She was booked and fingerprinted and charged. It all, like much of Angie's life, had a dream-like quality. She was just walking through it—as if her life was a TV show and she was simply watching it—the reality of her trouble not hitting her until the next day when her name appeared in the paper. The Cedar Rapids paper was read by everybody in her hometown. Angie called home and tried to explain. Her mother was in tears, her father enraged. They told her not, definitely *not,* to attend the family reunion two weekends hence.

Now it was two years later and Angie was living with Roy, who robbed banks and killed people when he thought it was necessary. She saw plainly now that he was never going to have the kind of money it took to make her a kept woman. Hell, he'd even hinted a few times that she should get another waitress job to help out with the rent and the food. Plus, there were the people he'd killed, three that she knew of for sure. The only one that really bothered her was his wife. Killing his wife was a real personal thing, and it scared Angie. Killing his own son scared her even more.

She spent the afternoon getting depressed about her bikinis. School would be out in a week. Swimming pools would be opening up. Time to flaunt her body. But this year there was too much of her body to flaunt. She'd put on twenty pounds. Ripples of cellulite could be seen on the back of her thighs. She wished now Roy hadn't talked her into getting his name tattooed on both her boobs.

At three-thirty, Jason came home. He was a skinny, sandy-haired kid with a lot of freckles and eyeglasses so thick they made you feel sorry for him. Kids like Jason always got picked on by other kids.

Something was wrong. He usually went to the refrigerator and got himself some milk and a piece of the pie Angie always kept on hand for both of them. Roy had a whiskey tooth, not a sweet tooth. Then Jason usually sat at the dining room table and watched *Batman*. But not today. He just muttered a greeting and went back to his little room and closed the door. Something really was wrong and she figured she knew what it was. She slipped a robe on over her bikini—you shouldn't be around him, your tits hangin' out that way, Roy said when-ever she wore a bikini around the trailer—and went back to his room and knocked gently. She could never figure out what he thought of her. He was almost always polite but never more than that.

"I'm asleep," he said.

She giggled. "If you were asleep, you couldn't say 'I'm asleep.' "

"I just don't feel like talkin', Angie."

She decided to risk it. "You heard us talkin' last night, didn't you, Jason?"

There was a long silence. "No."

"About your mom." No.

"About what happened to her."

There was another long silence. "He killed her. I heard him say so."

So Roy was right. The kid *had* heard.

She opened the door and went in. He lay on the bed. He

still had his sneakers on. A Spawn comic book lay across his chest. Sunlight angled in through the dirty window on the west wall and picked out the blond highlights in his hair.

She went over and sat down next to him. The springs made a noise. She tried not to think about her weight, or how her bikinis fit her. She was definitely going on a diet. She was going to be a kept woman, and one thing a kept woman had to do was keep her body good.

She said, "I just wanted you to know that I didn't have nothin' to do with it, what he did, I mean."

"Yeah," he said. "I know."

"And I also wanted you to know that your daddy isn't a bad man."

"Yes, he is."

"Sometimes he is. But not all the time."

"He broke your rib, didn't he?"

"He didn't mean to hit me that hard. He was just drunk was all. If he'd been sober, he wouldn't have hit me that hard."

"They say in school that a man shouldn't hit a woman at all."

"Well," she said, "you know what your daddy says about schools. That they're run by Jews and gays and colored people."

He stared at her. "I'm gonna turn him in."

She got scared. "Oh, honey, don't you *ever* say that to your daddy." She knew that Roy was looking for an excuse, any excuse, to kill Jason. "Promise me you won't. He'd get so mad he'd—"

She didn't need to finish her sentence. She sensed that the kid knew what she was talking about.

She said, "Is that a good comic book?"

"Not as good as Batman."

"Then how come you don't get Batman?"

"I already read it for this month."

"Oh."

She leaned forward and kissed him on the forehead. She'd never done that before. He was a nice kid. "You remember what I said now. You never say anything in front of your daddy about turnin' him in. You hear me?"

"Yeah, I guess so."

"You take a nap now."

She stood up.

Her mother had once said, "You give a man plenty of starch and a good piece of meat, he'll never complain about you or your cookin'." Angie had told this to Roy once and he'd grinned at her and pawed one of her breasts and said, "All depends on what kind of meat you're talkin' about." At the time, Angie had found his remark hilarious.

There was nothing to smile about as she made the Kraft cheese and macaroni while the pork chops sizzled in the oven. He was going to kill his own son. She couldn't get over it. His own son.

Forty-five minutes later, the three of them ate dinner. As always, Jason said grace to himself the way his mom had taught him. While he did this, Roy made a face and rolled his eyes. Little sissy son-of-a-bitch, he'd drunkenly said to Jason one night, sayin' grace like that.

Roy said, "Guess what I found today?"

Angie said, "What?"

"I was talkin' to the boy."

"Oh," Angie said, irritated with his tone of voice. "Pardon me for living."

She got up from the table and carried her dishes to the sink.

"Guess what I found today?" Roy said to Jason.

"What?"

"A real great spot for fishin'."

"Oh."

"For you and me. I always wanted to teach you how to fish."

"I thought you *hated* to fish," Jason said.

"Not anymore. I love fishin', don't I, babe?"

"Yeah," Angie said from the sink, where she was cleaning off her plate. "He loves fishin'."

Angie knew immediately that Roy had figured out how to kill the kid. He hated fishing, and even more he hated to do anything with the kid.

After supper, Jason went into his room. Most kids would be out playing in the warm spring night. Not Jason. He had a little twelve-inch TV in there and he had a lot of X-Files novels, too. He was well set up.

While she was doing the dishes, and Roy was sitting at the table nursing a Hamms from the bottle and watching some skin on the Playboy Channel, she said, "You're gonna do it."

"Yes, I am."

"He's your own flesh and blood."

He came over and pressed against her. He had a hard-on. Seems he always had a hard-on. She didn't have no complaints in that department. He groped her and kissed her neck and said, "We're free kind of people, Angie. Free. And with the kid along, we'll never be free. Especially with what he knows about us. One phone call from him and we'll be in the slammer."

"But he's your own son."

Jason's door opened. He went to the john. Roy said, "You let me take care of it."

Twenty minutes later, Roy and Jason left. She couldn't

think of any way to stop them without coming right out and warning Jason about what was going on.

She paced. She paced and gunned whiskey from a Smurfs glass. She was so agitated her heart felt like thunder in her chest and every few minutes her right arm jerked grotesquely.

And then she remembered the gun. She didn't even know what kind of gun it was. One of her lawyer friends had given it to her once when one of her old boyfriends was hassling her. She'd shot it a few times. She knew how to use it. She kept it in the bureau underneath the crotchless panties Roy had bought her, his joke always being that he'd personally eaten the crotch out of them.

She got the gun and she went after them. Her only thought was the river. About half a mile on the other side of some hardwoods was a cliff and below it fast water that ran to a dam near Cedar Rapids. One time they'd been walking and Roy said it was a perfect place to throw a body. His cellmate, a lifer Roy had a lot of respect for, had said that while bodies did occasionally wash up right away, there was a better chance they'd give you a five-, six-day head start from the law.

The dying day was indigo in the sky, indigo and salmon pink and mauve spreading like a stain beneath a few north-easterly thunderheads and a biting wind that tasted of rain. Rainstorms always scared her. When she was little, she'd always hidden in the closet, her two older sisters laughing at her, scaredy-pants, scaredy-pants. But she didn't care. She'd hidden anyway.

The way she found them, they were sitting on a picnic table near the cliff, father and son, just talking. Darkness was slowly making them grainy, and soon would make them invisible.

Roy said, "What the hell you doing here?"

"She can be here if she wants to," Jason said.

She smiled. The kid liked her and that made her feel good.

"I guess I need to go to the bathroom," Jason said.

He walked over to the hardwoods and disappeared.

"I was afraid you already did something to him," Angie said.

He looked at her. Shrugged. "It's harder than I thought it would be."

"He's your own flesh and blood."

"Yeah, yeah, I guess that's it. I started to do it a couple times but I couldn't go through with it. I mean, it's not like shootin' a stranger or anything."

"Let's go back."

He shook his head. "Oh, no. You go back alone."

"But if you can't do it, why you want to stay out here?"

"I didn't say I *can't* do it. I just said it's harder than I thought it was. It's just gonna take me a little time is all. Now, you get that sweet ass of yours back home and wait for me. We'll be pullin' out tonight."

"Pullin' out?"

They could see Jason coming back toward them.

"Yeah," Roy said in a whispering voice, "school'll be askin' questions, him not around anymore. Better off pullin' out tonight."

Jason walked up. "Dad tell you there's twenty-pound fish in that river?"

"Yeah," she said, "that's what he said."

"Angie's got to get back home. She's makin' us a surprise."

"A surprise?" Jason said, excited. "What kinda surprise?"

"Well, if she tells ya, it won't be much of a surprise, will it?"

Jason grinned. "No, I guess not."

"You head home, babe," Roy said. "We'll be up'n a while."

She wanted to argue but you didn't argue with Roy. You didn't argue and win, anyway. And you got bruises and bumps and breaks for *not* winning.

"Guess I better go," she said.

"I can't wait to see the surprise," Jason said.

She went back but she didn't go home. She stood inside the hardwoods, inside the shadows, inside the night, and watched them.

He couldn't do it. That's what she was hoping. That when it came right down to it, he just couldn't do it. She said a couple of prayers.

But he did it. Pulled the gun out, grabbed Jason by the shoulder and started dragging him across the grassy space between picnic table and cliff.

All this was instinct: her running, her screaming. Roy looked real pissed when he saw her. He got distracted from the kid and the kid tried wrestling himself away, swinging his arms wild, trying to kick, trying to bite.

Roy didn't have any warning about her gun. She got up close to him and jerked it out of the back pocket of her Levi's and killed him point-blank. Three bullets in the side of the head.

He went over on his side and shit his pants before he hit the ground. The smell was awful.

The weird thing was how the kid reacted. You'd think he'd be grateful that she'd killed the son-of-a-bitch. But he knelt next to Roy and wailed and rocked back and forth and held a dead cold white hand in his hand and then wailed some more. Maybe, she thought, maybe it was because his mom was dead, too. Maybe losin' both your folks, maybe it was too much to handle, even if your own flesh-and-blood dad *had* tried to kill you.

She dragged Roy over and pushed him off the cliff into the river. The stars were on the water tonight and the choppy waves glistened.

She dragged the boy away. He fought at first, biting, kicking, wrestling, and all. She let him have a good hard slap, though, and that settled him down. He kept cryin' but he did what she told him. "How you doin'?"

"All right."

"You hungry?"

"Sort of, I guess."

"You'll like Colorado. Wait till you see the mountains."

"You didn't have to kill him."

"He was gonna kill *you*."

He didn't say anything for a long time. They were nearing the Nebraska border. The land was getting flatter. Cows, crying with prairie sorrow, tossed in their earthen beds, while night birds collected chorus-like in the trees, making the leafy branches thrum with their song. It was nice with the windows rolled down and all the summery Midwest roaring in your ears.

Sixty-three miles before they hit the border, just after ten o'clock, they found the Empire Motel, one of those 1950s jobs with the office in the middle and eight stucco-sided rooms fanned out on either side.

Angie rented a room and bought a bunch of candy and potato chips from the vending machine. She rented a sci-fi video from the manager for Jason.

She got him into the shower and then into bed and played the movie for him. He didn't last long. He was asleep in no time. She turned out the lights and got into bed herself. She was tired. Or thought she was, anyway. But she couldn't sleep. She lay there and thought about Roy and about when she was a little girl and about being a kept woman. It had to happen for her someday. It just had to. Then she remembered what she'd looked like in those bikinis. God, she really had to go on a diet.

She lay like this for an hour. Then she heard car doors opening and male laughter. She decided to go peek out the window. Two nice-looking, nicely dressed guys were carrying a suitcase each into a room two doors away. They were driving this just-huge new Lincoln. Sight of them made her agitated. She wanted a drink and to hear some music. Maybe dance a little. And laugh. She needed a good laugh.

Fifteen minutes later, she was fixed up pretty good, white tank top and red short-shorts, the ones where her cheeks were exposed to erotic perfection, her hair all done up nice, and enough perfume so that she smelled really good.

The kid wouldn't miss her. He'd be fine. He'd be sleeping and the door would be locked and he'd be just fine.

Their names were Jim Durbin and Mike Brady. They were from Cedar Rapids and they owned a couple of computer stores and they were going to open a big new one in Denver. Ordinarily, Jim would fly but Mike was scared to fly. And ordinarily, they would stay in a nicer motel than this but they couldn't find anything else on the road. Her excuse for knocking on their door this late was the front office didn't have a cigarette machine and she was out and she heard them still up and she wondered if either of them had a few cigarettes they'd loan her. Jim said he didn't smoke but Mike did. Jim said he'd been trying for years to get Mike to quit. How do you like that? Jim said. Guy doesn't mind risking lung cancer every day of his life but he won't get on an airplane?

They had a nice bottle of I. W. Harper and invited her in.

It was obvious Mike was interested in her. Jim was married. Mike was just going through a divorce he called "painful." He said his wife ended up running off with this doctor she was on this charity committee with. Jim said Mike needed a good woman to rebuild Mike's self-esteem. That was a word Angie heard a lot. She liked the daytime talk shows and they talked a lot about self-esteem. There was a transvestite prostitute on just last week, as a matter of fact, and Angie felt sorry for the poor thing. He/she said that's all he/she was looking for, self-esteem.

Angie got sort of drunk and spent her time talking to Mike while Jim took a shower and got ready for bed. Angie could tell he was taking a real long time to give Mike and her a chance to be alone. And then they were making out and his hands were all over her and then she was down on her knees next to his bed and doing him and he was gasping and groaning and bucking and just going crazy and it made her feel powerful and wonderful to make a man this happy, especially a broken-hearted one.

When Jim came back, wearing a red terry-cloth robe and rubbing his crew cut with a white towel, Angie and Mike were sitting in chairs and having another drink.

"So, what's going on?" Jim said.

"Well," Mike said, and he looked like a teenager, excited and nervous at the same time, "I was going to ask Angie if she'd like to come to Denver with me. Spend a couple of weeks while we get the grand opening all set up and everything."

Jim said, still rubbing his crew cut with the white towel, "This is a guy who does everything first-class, Angie, let me tell you. You should see his condo. The view of the city. Unbelievable."

"You like Jet Skiing?" Mike said.

"Sure," Angie said, though she wasn't exactly sure what it was.

"Well, I've got *two* Jet Skis and they're a ball. Believe me, we could have a lot of fun. You could stay at my condo and do what you like during the day—shop or whatever—and then at night, we'll get together again."

Jim said, "God, Angie, you're a miracle worker. This sounds like my old buddy Mike Brady. I haven't heard him sound this happy in three or four years."

Mike grinned. "Maybe I'm in love."

And he leaned over and slid his arm around Angie's neck and gave her a big whiskey kiss on the mouth.

All she could think of was how strange it was. Maybe she'd met the man who was going to make her into a kept woman. And this one wasn't married, either. He could marry her somewhere down the line.

She said, "Wait till I tell Jason."

Mike gave her a funny look. "Jason? Who's Jason?"

Jim came over, too. "Yeah, who's Jason?"

"Oh, sort of my stepson, I guess you'd say."

"You're traveling with a kid?" Mike said.

"Yeah."

Mike didn't have to say anything. It was all in his face. He'd been outlining an orgy of activities and she went and ruined it all with reality. A kid. A fucking kid.

"Oh," Mike said, finally.

"He's a real nice kid," Angie said. "Real quiet and every-thing."

"I'm sure he's a nice kid, Angie," Jim said. "But I don't think that's what Mike had in mind. Nothing against kids, you understand. I've got two of my own and Mike's got three."

"I love kids," Mike said, as if somebody had accused him otherwise.

"He wouldn't be any trouble," Angie said. "He really wouldn't."

Mike and Jim looked at each other and Jim said, looking at Angie now, "You know what we should do? Why don't we take your phone number, you know where you're staying in Omaha and everything, and then Mike can give you a call when he gets settled into his condo?"

Mike didn't have nerve enough to say good-bye so Jim was doing it for him.

A ball and chain, she remembered Roy said about Jason. Mike wasn't going to call. Jim was just saying that. And she'd be somewhere in Omaha, maybe with a waitress job or something. And pretty soon school would roll around and she'd have to worry about school clothes and getting him enrolled in a new school and everything. While somebody else would be living with Mike in his Denver condo, and Jet Skiing, whatever that was, and using Mike's American Express to buy new clothes and stuff.

She said, "You know if there's a river around here somewhere?"

"A river?" Jim said.

"Yes," she said. "A river."

Next morning at seven A.M. she knocked on the door. A sleepy pajamaed Jim opened it. "Hey," he said. "How's it goin'?" He sounded a little leery of seeing her. He'd obviously hoped they'd put the Denver matter to rest last night.

"Guess what?" she said.

"What?"

"I said I was sort of Jason's stepmother? Well, actually, I'm his aunt. My sister lives about ten miles from here and has troubles with depression. She wanted me to take him for a while but she stopped by the room here real early this morning and picked him up. Said she was feeling a lot better."

Mike could be seen over Jim's shoulder now. He said, excited, "So you don't have the kid anymore?"

"Free, white and twenty-one," she said.

"You're going to Denver!" he said.

Jim said, "I'm going to get some breakfast down the road. I'll be back in an hour or so."

He got dressed quick and left.

They did it their first time right in Mike's mussed bed. Only once or twice did she think of the kid, and how she'd smothered him in the room. She hadn't had any trouble finding the river. She had to give it to Roy. The ball-and-chain business. She had liked the kid but he really was a ball and chain.

A few hours later, they left for Denver. That night, they had spare ribs for supper at a roadside place. They drank a lot of wine, or vino, as Jim kept calling it, and Mike as a joke licked some of the rib sauce off her fingers. She was scared about later, when she went to sleep. Maybe she'd have night-mares about the kid. But she snuggled up to Mike real good and after they made love, they lay in the darkness sharing his cigarette and talking about Denver and she ended up not having any dreams at all.

Copyright cont.

"Such A Good Writer" Copyright © 2000 by Richard
Laymon.
"All These Condemned" Copyright © 2000 by Ed Gorman.
"A Girl Like You" Copyright © 2000 by Ed Gorman.
"The Way It Used To Be" Copyright © 1998 by Ed Gorman.
First appeared in *1998 Revolver*.
"A New Man" Copyright © 2000 by Ed Gorman.
"Judgment" Copyright © 1993 by Ed Gorman. First appeared
in *Monsters in Our Midst*.
"Ghosts" Copyright © 1997 by Ed Gorman. First appeared in
Dark Whispers.
"That Day at Eagle's Point" Copyright © 1996 by Ed
Gorman. First appeared in *Guilty As Charged*.
"Such A Good Girl" Copyright © 1999 by Ed Gorman. First
appeared in *Subterranean Gallery*.
"Aftermath" Copyright © 2000 by Ed Gorman.
"Eye of the Beholder" Copyright © 1996 by Ed Gorman. First
appeared in *The Dwyer Trilogy* (CD Publications).
"Angie" Copyright © 1998 by Ed Gorman. First appeared in
999.